A Secret Christmas

J.E.B. Spredemann

Published in Indiana by *Blessed Publishing*.

www.jenniferspredemann.com

All Scripture quotations are taken from the *King James Version* of the *Holy Bible*.

Cover design by *iCreate Designs* ©

Original ISBN: 978-1-940492-37-7

Second Edition ISBN: 978-1-940492-92-6

10 9 8 7 6 5 4 3 2 1

BOOKS BY J.E.B. SPREDEMANN

(*J. Spredemann)

AMISH GIRLS SERIES

Joanna's Struggle

Danika's Journey

Chloe's Revelation

Susanna's Surprise

Annie's Decision

Abigail's Triumph

Brooke's Quest

Leah's Legacy

NOVELS*

*Love Impossible**

*Amish by Accident**

*An Unforgivable Secret** - Amish Secrets 1

*A Secret Encounter** - Amish Secrets 2

*A Secret of the Heart** - Amish Secrets 3

*An Undeniable Secret** - Amish Secrets 4

A Secret Sacrifice - Amish Secrets 5

A Secret of the Soul* - Amish Secrets 6

Learning to Love – Saul's Story* (Sequel to Chloe's Revelation – adult novella)

Englisch on Purpose (Prequel to Amish by Accident)*

NOVELLAS

A Christmas of Mercy – Amish Girls Holiday

Christmas in Paradise – (Final book in Amish by Accident trilogy)

A Secret Christmas – Amish Secrets 2.5

NOVELETTES*

Cindy's Story* – An Amish Fairly Tale Novelette 1

Rosabelle's Story* – An Amish Fairly Tale Novelette 2

COMING 2019 (Lord Willing)

An Amish Betrayal (March 2019)

An Amish Reward (June 2019

An Amish Deception (September 2019)

The Unexpected Gift (November 2019)

Unofficial Glossary of Pennsylvania Dutch Words

Ach – Oh

Aldi – Girlfriend

Bann – Shunning

Bopplin – Babies

Daed/Dat – Dad

Dawdi Haus – A small house intended to house parents or grandparents

Denki – Thanks

Der Herr – The Lord

Dochder – Daughter

Englischer – A non-Amish person

Gott – God

Grossdochder – Granddaughter

Mammi – Grandmother

Gut – Good

Jah – Yes

Kapp – Amish head covering

Kinner – Children

Mamm – Mom

Ordnung – Rules of the Amish community

Schatzi – Sweetheart

Sehr gut – Very good

Characters in *A Secret Christmas*

The Bender Family

Joe — Protagonist

Anna — Joe's wife

Mary — oldest daughter

Little Joe — son

Mandy — daughter

Others

Harv — Joe's friend, honorary uncle to Bender children, character in *A Secret Encounter*

Mammi – Anna's grandmother

Candace Dixon — Protagonist, *Englisch* woman from California

Jackie — Candace's oldest daughter

Maddie — Candace's youngest daughter

Taylor — Joe and Anna's *Englisch* neighbor

Jacob and Rachel Schrock — Anna's cousins

Jonathan Fisher — Proprietor of Fisher's Furniture, key character throughout the *Amish Girls Series*

Danika Yoder—Herbalist, Protagonist in *Danika's Journey* (Amish Girls Series – book 2)

Linda — Owner of Threads of Beauty

To anyone who has lost a spouse or close loved one... Take comfort in the words of Jesus, "I will never leave thee, nor forsake thee."

Author's Note

It should be noted that the Amish/Mennonite people and their communities differ one from another. There are, in fact, no two Amish communities exactly alike. It is this premise on which this book is written. I have taken cautious steps to assure the authenticity of Amish practices and customs. Old Order Amish and New Order Amish may be portrayed in this work of fiction and may differ from some communities.

We, as *Englischers*, can learn a lot from the Plain People and their simple way of life. Their hard work, close-knit family life, and concern for others are to be applauded. As the Lord wills, may this special culture continue to be respected and remain so for many centuries to come, and may the light of God's salvation reach their hearts.

PROLOGUE

Pennsylvania, Early December

Joseph Bender's head shot up at the piercing scream that ricocheted through the air. *Was that Mary?* He immediately dropped the lead line to his mare and bolted toward the house.

"Joe? What's wrong?" Harvey meandered out of the barn, his expression light as usual but a hint of concern manifested in his eyes.

Joe shook his head. "I don't know, Harv. But I'm certain that was Mary who just screamed." He threw the screen door open and rushed inside. Moisture gathered in his palms and an uneasiness settled in the pit of his stomach as the door slammed shut behind him.

"Anna?" He entered the kitchen. His wife was nowhere in sight. He ran to young Mary's bedroom but found it empty. "Anna? Where are you?"

"I'm in here. In the bathroom." The distress in her voice caused his heart to lurch.

He poked his head through the bathroom door and his gaze met his wife's. "What's going on, *Schatzi*? Why was Mary screaming?"

"I don't know if she had a nightmare or if it was because of her fever. She's been a little out of sorts since we returned from her doctor visit, but nothing like now. She feels pretty hot."

Joe came close and touched the back of his hand to his daughter's forehead. His heart felt like melted wax when he noticed Mary's lethargic countenance, a stark contrast from her normal happy extroverted self.

"You're right, she's burning up." Did Anna recognize the worry his tone conveyed?

He kneeled next to the bathtub, reached into the cool water surrounding Mary, dipped a washcloth into it, and then placed it on Mary's forehead. "Does that feel better, *liebling*?"

Mary attempted to smile and speak but all that passed her lips was a groan.

"Did you check her temperature?" He frowned.

Anna shook her head. "Not since earlier this morning. It was a hundred and one then. The thermometer is in Mary's room on her dresser."

He briefly squeezed Anna's hand, communicating to his wife that everything would be alright. He just wished his heart felt the same confidence his action exuded.

"I'll get it." Joe turned toward the bedroom and silently pleaded with God on Mary's behalf. *Please don't take her yet, Lord. Five years isn't long enough. We can't lose her. You know how much Anna and I love her.*

Tears were rare for him, but once in a while he couldn't help their formation. This was one of those times. He shoved the tear away with the pad of his thumb. He couldn't let Anna or the children see his distress—they needed his strength, his leadership.

He took a cleansing breath and stepped back into the bathroom. He handed the thermometer to Anna. "Where are the *kinner*?"

"They're napping." She held the thermometer under Mary's tongue.

"I'm surprised Mary's scream didn't awaken them."

"You know they can sleep through anything." She pulled the thermometer out of Mary's mouth and frowned.

"What? What is it?"

"A hundred and four. I didn't expect it to still be so high. She's been in the cool water for almost ten minutes now." She brought a cup of water to Mary's mouth. "Drink, *lieb*."

Their daughter did as told, but Joseph could see she was struggling to get it down. Her eyelids seemed heavy with exhaustion. "We've got to keep her hydrated."

"She can't drink much."

"I think we should take her to the ER. At least they can give her an IV."

Anna frowned. "I'm scheduled to work today. I'll need to call Linda and let her know I won't be able to make it."

"Harv can go in for you. And I'm sure *Mammi* won't mind watching the little ones for us."

"You're sure?"

"Yep. I'll stop by the *dawdi* house and talk to *Mammi,* then go call the neighbor to see if he can give us a ride. We'll have him drop Harv off at Threads of Beauty after he takes us to the hospital."

"Sounds like a plan. I think I'll just keep Mary in the bath until Taylor arrives, then we can wrap her in a towel." She looked to him for approval.

He grimaced, not caring for the idea, then offered a quick nod. "They'll probably have her change into a hospital gown as soon as we arrive anyway."

Joseph rushed out the door, not bothering to keep it from slamming shut behind him.

~

"Doctor, what do you think is wrong with her?" Joseph glanced down at Mary. She appeared so frail and helpless lying in the large hospital bed with an IV strapped to her arm. At least she was sleeping now.

The doctor rubbed his chin. "You said she had a check-up recently?"

"Yes, just this morning."

"Hmm...And she was fine then?"

Joseph frowned. "*Jah*, I think so." He looked to Anna for confirmation.

"That's peculiar."

"What do you think is wrong with her, doctor?" Joseph watched as the doctor checked Mary's vital signs.

"It's difficult to say for sure. A fever can be indicative of many different things."

"Like?"

"Could be the flu." He moved his stethoscope to Mary's chest. "I hear some congestion. It's most likely just an upper respiratory infection."

"With a fever?"

"That's just a sign that her body is fighting off whatever she has. The danger with fevers is when dehydration is present as well. But she's hooked up to an IV now, so that shouldn't be a problem for Mary. You need not worry, Mr. Bender, your daughter should be fine soon enough."

"So, this is normal?" Joe frowned.

"It happens quite often." He nodded.

"Mary has had very few sicknesses," Anna interjected, stroking Mary's hand.

"Then count your blessings." The doctor shrugged. "Your daughter is certainly not the first to get sick. I wouldn't worry."

Joe expelled a relieved sigh. "*Gut.* Thank you, doctor."

Although he appreciated the doctor's confidence and hoped he was correct, Joe's agreement with the doctor betrayed his true concerns. *Jah,* the doctor didn't seem troubled, but this was *their* Mary. Mary, who was typically happy-go-lucky and full of zest. Mary, who rarely got anything more than a sniffle.

He watched the doctor leave the room, then glanced at his wife. He read the distress in her face, saw the unshed tears of worry in her eyes. He pulled her close and kissed the top of her head.

Then he surveyed Mary again, whose cheeks were flushed bright pink. She looked so small. So frail. So vulnerable.

Never in his life had he felt so helpless. He was supposed to be the leader of this family. The provider. The protector. Yet, in this moment, he felt like an utter failure.

Please, Gott, help Mary. Help us.

ONE

December, A Year Prior

Joseph's face illuminated as he watched his daughter. One by one, Mary removed the wrapped gifts from a large decorated plastic sack, and handed them to each homeless person present. The joy on his daughter's face brought happiness to his own. *If only Anna could be here to see this!*

He looked on as his daughter leaned close and whispered in one of the transients' ears. Joe didn't have to guess what she was saying, he already knew.

The man's clothes were dirty and torn, much like Joe's had been less than a decade ago when he and Anna first met, and he wore a scraggly beard. But none of that fazed his Mary. The man stared back at her with wide eyes, then flitted a glance toward Joseph. He nodded to the man. The man looked back at Mary and gave a slight nod and she wrapped her tiny arms around his neck. When the man smiled in response, Joe noted several missing teeth. Fortunately, he still had all of his.

As the man opened the gift of a hat, scarf, and mittens, Mary beamed with pride. Joseph overheard her say, "I helped Momma make those! But the hug was from Jesus."

Typically, Amish children didn't learn English until they began school. But since Harvey had been a part of their household, they'd spoken both English and Pennsylvania German in the home since before she'd been born. At four years old, she was already bilingual speech-wise.

The man stared at Joseph, then rose from his chair. He approached Joe with Mary's dainty hand leading the way.

"Is she your daughter?" The man gestured to young Mary.

"Yes, she is." Joe found it difficult to keep the pride out of his voice. His Mary had so many of her momma's traits, she often reminded him of Anna.

"She's a sweetheart. You are very lucky to have her." The man smiled down at Mary, who now held Joe's hand.

"Yes. The Lord has given me many blessings. She is one of them." Joseph bent down and whispered in Mary's ear. He then watched as she went and sought out Harvey. "About seven years ago, I was living on the streets myself."

"Oh, really?" The man rubbed his beard and appeared to be appraising Joe's Amish attire. "I never would have guessed."

"It was a dark time for me. A lot of struggles. I battled many personal demons." He stuck out his hand. "My name's Joe, by the way."

"Nice to meet you, Joe. I'm Ralph." The man accepted his greeting and nodded.

"I can relate to hardship. It wasn't until I met my wife, then Jesus, that things started to change."

"I once had a wife. Cathy." Ralph's chin began to quiver and he immediately quit talking.

Joe waited for him to continue.

"She left me."

"I'm sorry to hear that."

"It was my own fault. I couldn't quit drinkin'."

Joe knew that feeling of self-deprecation all too well. He clasped the man's shoulder. "God can help you with that. He can give you a brand-new life."

Ralph shook his head. "I don't know. I've tried praying before."

"It's more than just a prayer." Joe frowned, silently asking God for His leading. "He did it for me. He can do it for you too."

"How?"

"Well, if you're serious, we have a program you can go through. It's helped a lot of people put their darkest days behind them. But you have to be willing."

"I'd do anything to get my wife back."

Joe knew that Ralph's getting his wife back was not the greatest concern, and he was confident his new friend would soon discover this fact. But if this was his current motivation, it would be enough for now. "Great. Come to the meeting room this Friday night at seven."

"Will you be there?"

"I sure will, unless God has a change of plans."

~

"Hey, Joe." Harv slung his arm around Joseph's shoulders. "May I have a word with you?"

"Sure. Let's sit." They sat in a place where he had a clear view of Mary. She sat eating a bowl of soup with one of the female volunteers. "What's on your mind?"

"Do you remember that man that came in a few weeks back? He wore a blue sweatshirt and a ball cap?"

"Yeah. Wasn't his name Larry? He was in and out pretty quickly. I really didn't even have time to sit down and have a decent conversation with him."

"That's too bad." Harv shook his head. "Heard he took his own life yesterday."

Joe frowned. "Oh no. Really?"

"Yep. He OD'd on pain meds."

Joe rubbed his chest. "That hurts my heart."

"I know. But we can't save everybody." Harv patted Joe's back.

"I know. Sometimes... Do you ever feel like you're not doing all that you could be doing? When I hear things like that I just feel like I'm not doing enough, like I'm not making a difference," Joe lamented.

"What are you talking about, Joe?"

"Well, I read about these people—missionaries in foreign countries—how they are horribly persecuted and sacrifice their lives for the Saviour. Some of them even leading hundreds or thousands to Christ." He frowned. "Then I look around at what I'm doing. I don't know. I just feel like it's not enough."

"Remember, it is God who gives the increase."

"I know."

"They that compare themselves among themselves are not wise." Harv scratched his white beard. "It seems to me like God has a special calling for each person. I agree that missionaries are great and we need them. But not everyone who is a child of God has to go to a foreign field. Lost souls are everywhere, Joe. Don't think that your calling, your sacrifice, is any less important."

Harv continued, "You are raisin' your *kinner* to serve God. Just look at sweet little Mary over there. That is important. You are being a good husband to Anna. That is important. You are helping strangers at the shelter find their way to Jesus. That is important. Walk the path God has laid out for *you*."

"I think I should be doing more."

"Then do more. But don't forget about your family—they need you. They are your *first* ministry." Harvey stared at Joe and he knew a spiritual lesson was coming. "Remember the prophet Jeremiah? He preached for a hundred years and didn't get one convert. Do you think his reward in Heaven was any less or that God was displeased with him?"

"Probably not."

"That's right, because he was doing what God called him to do. We do our best to do our part and leave the results up to God. Do you feel like this is what God has called you to do?"

"*Jah.*"

"Then you have no need to feel ashamed. Just do it with your whole heart."

"*Jah.* Okay." Joe nodded.

TWO

California Central Valley

Candace Dixon stared at the name on the computer screen, then reviewed the results of her genealogical search for the second time. It couldn't be, could it?

She painstakingly studied page after page one more time. Perhaps she'd missed something...

She hadn't. The results were clear.

No death certificate. Which meant...

Did she even want to ponder the possibility? Did she even want to open herself up to the emotions that would no doubt consume her until she found the answers she sought? Did she even *want* the answers?

Yes, she did, she realized. She couldn't just ignore the results. If they were indeed correct, that meant she had family out there. Somewhere. Flesh and blood relatives whom she'd never met.

The thought was astounding. Unbelievable, actually.

For better or worse, she had to find out.

~

Joseph maneuvered the horse and buggy into the driveway, thrilled to catch a glimpse of his wife as she hung laundry on the line. Little Joe played with a cat near Anna's feet. He'd never tire of coming home to his beloved. After six years of marriage, his heart still filled with gratitude each day he returned home to her. Marrying Anna had been a dream he'd never imagined would ever come true, yet here they were.

Gott had truly been good, showering him with blessings he didn't deserve. He never wanted to take those blessings for granted. He'd been on the other side and had seen mankind at his worst. It was a place he never wished to return to.

A warm breeze kicked up as he dismounted the buggy. The weather had been surprising for this time of year. Normally, they'd have snow on the ground by now. But instead, they enjoyed temperatures in the sixties. It hardly even felt like winter. But he knew the cold weather would eventually come, most likely with a vengeance. Even so, he looked forward to snowy days when he'd spend a little more time at home. He looked forward to making snowmen and sledding with the children. He looked forward to cuddling by the fire with his gorgeous wife after everyone else in the household retired for the evening.

Fortunately, his paying job was accommodating and his work at the homeless shelter was voluntary. He'd juggled the two jobs for several years now. His volunteer job at the shelter brought him a sense of satisfaction that money could never buy. And his day job, online marketing for several local businesses, had provided for his family's material needs.

He enjoyed the fact that he was able to bring Mary to the shelter with him. He and Anna felt it was important that their *kinner* learned compassion at an early age, lest they grow up to become self-centered and apathetic toward their fellow man. It brought him immense satisfaction to see young Mary's tender heart when it came to helping out the less fortunate.

His day job was atypical for an Amish man. Each time he shared what his occupation was with another human being, whether they were Amish or *Englisch*, they always had the same reaction, which typically went something like this, "I didn't think the Amish were allowed to use computers." Or "You can use electricity?" It was always accompanied by a confounded expression.

Each time, he'd inform them that every Amish church district varied according to the *Ordnung* they chose to follow. And even though they followed a specific *Ordnung* now, it didn't mean they'd still be adhering to the same set of rules ten years down the road. No, their *Ordnung* changed with the times and could vary with each situation that presented itself.

As a matter of fact, Joseph's occupation had been one instance that had come before the leaders and had been voted on by the church members in good standing. He'd caused quite a stir among the brethren. Not everyone was for it but, thankfully, he'd been able to keep his occupation. With certain stipulations, of course. He hated to think that the years he'd spent in college and at his former job—when he'd been shunned from the Swartzentrubers before he joined his present Amish district—would be wasted.

They eventually agreed to allow him the use of the computer away from the home, reasoning that other Amish in the community used electric and other *Englisch* trappings when they went off to their day jobs. Originally, he'd conducted his business from the local library. Since then, Linda at Threads of Beauty, the quilt shop where Anna worked part time, had graciously allowed him to set up a small office in one of the rooms in the back of her store.

When he'd first joined Bishop Hostettler's district, he'd been amazed at the differences between the Amish group Anna belonged to and the Swartzentruber Amish sect he'd grown up in. The differences were like night and day. His former church would have *never* allowed an occupation like Joe's. Now that he'd been a part of the Hostettler district, he couldn't imagine *ever* going back to the strict ways of his former fellowship.

He'd been thankful that his folks had joined a more liberal Amish group as well, although they'd thought the Hostettler district a little too lax for their liking. The group he'd grown up in had been controlling to the extreme. He appreciated the fact that they practiced forgiveness, but not at the expense of others' well-being. He'd dealt with that firsthand as a young man.

As he unhitched the horse from the buggy, Harv helped Mary down. Anna's eyes brightened and she came near, planting her hands on his chest. He glanced over her shoulder and smiled at

Little Joe, now contently sitting inside the empty laundry basket. Mary had joined him and now cooed to her younger brother and played with the kitty.

"I missed you," she smiled.

He dropped the line in his hand and pulled her close, cupping her chin with his fingers. As his lips met his wife's, all the cares of the day seemed to just slip away into oblivion.

"Mm..." He held her for several minutes, lingering as long as time and circumstances allowed. When their little one squealed with delight, only then did they break apart.

His hand splayed over Anna's flat abdomen and her sparkling eyes met his. There was nothing more intimate than the bond between a husband and wife. Only the two of them knew of the secret she kept within. Hopefully, by next year at this time, they'd be adding another little one to their precious family. He whispered sweet nothings in her ear and she rewarded him with the laughter he loved.

"You two act like you're still courtin'!" Harv bellowed with a chuckle.

"We are." Joe winked at Anna and finally relinquished her to her duties. "And what's wrong with that, Harv?"

"Ain't nothin' wrong with it. Just makin' an observation is all." He shook his head. "Better hope *Mammi* don't catch you two out here smoochin' in front of the youngins."

Joe waved Harv's concern away. "*Ach*, there isn't a married couple alive who hasn't kissed in front of other people."

"Not too sure about that."

"Well, *I* intend to enjoy my *fraa* whenever and wherever I please. And if anyone has anything to say about it, they can look up Proverbs chapter five."

He heard Anna's gasp from the porch. "Joseph Bender!"

He chuckled and held up his hands in surrender. "Hey, I'm just saying that enjoying my wife is Biblical. That's all. They can add Song of Solomon to their reading list while they're at it."

Harvey smirked and shook his head. "You're hopeless."

"Yep. Hopelessly in love with my wife." He looked over at Anna and winked at her just before she slipped into the house with the little ones.

He studied his friend. "What about you, Harv?"

"What do you mean?"

"Don't act like you don't know what I'm talking about." He pointed to Harv's chest. "You and *Mammi* have been flirting with each other for years."

Harv made a mock gasp and his hand flew to his heart, feigning innocence. "*Moi*? Flirting?"

18

"Yes, you." He shook his head and chuckled. "Are you ever going to ask *Mammi* out? You two aren't exactly spring chicks anymore."

"I ain't Amish. She is. End of story. Even if we *wanted* to pursue a relationship, it could never be."

"I wasn't Amish when I met Anna."

"Yeah, but that's different. You were born Amish. I, on the other hand, am a red-blooded, flag-waving American who served in and *still* believes in the military. In case you've forgotten."

"I haven't forgotten."

"I could never agree with the pacifist line of thinking. It goes against everything I've ever believed. And since you were quoting the Bible earlier, let me remind *you* that it says that those who bear the sword are the ministers of God." He pointed to Joe. "Which is why *all* me and *Mammi* can ever be is friends."

Joe's brow shot up. "And you're content with that?"

Harv sighed. "I have to be."

THREE

"I met someone today. It was a new guy I'd never seen at the shelter before." Joseph confided in Anna as he sipped his cup of after-dinner coffee.

"Really? What was his name?"

Joe smiled. He loved it when Anna took an interest in the day's events. "Ralph Ainsley."

She nodded. Most likely attempting to remember his name so she could add him to her prayer list. "Did he share his story with you?"

He nodded. "Some. He's battled a problem with alcohol for a while, it seems. Lost his family because of it."

Anna frowned. "That's too bad."

"He really wants to get his wife back. He didn't mention whether they were divorced or separated."

"That's sad. Did you invite him to attend the Reformers Unanimous meetings?"

"I did. He's planning on being there Friday night. I don't think he knows the Lord. I've already been praying for his salvation."

"Then that's what I'll pray for too. Not just for his, but for his family's as well."

"Good idea." Joe reached over and took his wife's hand in his. They'd tucked the children into bed a half hour ago. He loved this alone time with his wife every evening. "How was your day?"

"Pretty good. *Mammi* and I made up the pie crusts for the Christmas sale this weekend. On Friday night, we'll fill and bake them, so they're fresh for the customers."

"I'm glad Linda suggested that. It's kind of her to allow us to sell our goods in her store."

"I think she loves the fact that we always bring her a free pie. Although she always ends up buying stuff too. She says it brings customers in. They come in for the free dessert samples and end up purchasing a pie *and* a quilt." She eyed her husband. "Sounds like a marketing mastermind came up with that. You sure it was Linda's idea and not yours?"

"My lips are sealed." He zipped his lips and grinned.

"*Ach*, I knew it!"

"In all fairness, Linda *did* give me the idea initially. She said we needed to think of something more to bring in customers. You know I love to eat. What better way to lure people in than fresh home-baked desserts?"

"I always knew you were a genius."

"Only because I have a beautiful wife to inspire me."

She shook her head. "You lie. Your inspiration comes from *Der Herr*."

"Maybe so. But *you're* the one who bakes the pies." He kissed her cheek. "Which reminds me... You didn't happen to make any peanut butter and chocolate whoopie pies this time, did you?" Did he sound like he was begging? Because he felt like he was begging.

The twinkle in her eye revealed the truth.

"You did!"

"Maybe." She teased.

"I knew it. Have I ever told you that I love you?" He kissed her. "And that I'm so so glad I married you?" He kissed her again. "And that you're the best *fraa* ever?" And again.

Anna laughed. "I think you're overdoing it, *lieb*."

"Uh uh. Never." He leaned over and kissed her again before finally moving back. "Thank you, *Schatzi*."

"You know I love to see you happy." She winked.

"Happy, I am." He rubbed her shoulder. "What are we doing with the money this year?"

"We'll donate half of the proceeds to the shelter like usual, and we'll use the remainder for Christmas."

"That sounds *gut*."

"Which reminds me. I had an idea."

Joe rubbed his hands together. "I love to hear your ideas. What is it?"

"You know how Linda has that Christmas tree in the store with those paper angels on it? The ones that the prisoners fill out so that their children get gifts for Christmas?"

He nodded. "Yes, the Angel Tree program. I'm familiar with it."

"How would you feel about doing something like that at the shelter?"

"What do you mean? For the children of the homeless people?" He shook his head. "I think most of them may not know where their loved ones are."

"Maybe. But I'm sure some of them do." She shrugged.

"It's a good idea. But where would we put up the tree?"

"We could ask Taylor and some of our other *Englisch* friends if their church would like to sponsor one."

He considered her proposal.

"And if they're local families, we can deliver the gifts." She added. "Mary would love to be part of that."

Joe smiled. "I know she would. But what if they're not local?"

"We can just send them through the mail? I don't know. It's a thought."

"Not necessarily a bad one." He scratched his head. "Wait. I have an idea. What if it was an online thing too? I could ask the local businesses that I market for if we can add a giving box or giving tree to their websites."

"Do you think it would work?"

"Only one way to find out." Perhaps this was it. A way he could make even more of an impact for *Der Herr*. He stood up and reached for her hand. "Now let's go find those whoopie pies you're hiding from me."

FOUR

Candace sipped her coffee as she read the confusion on her adult daughters' expressions.

"Wait, Mom. You're going *where*?" Her eldest daughter, Jackie, frowned.

"Remember the wedding in Pennsylvania I told you about? My old high school friend that moved back East?"

"Oh, yeah. Okay. When will you be back? You're supposed to babysit for us next Friday, so don't forget."

"I'll be back in plenty of time for that." Candace batted her hand.

"We have our family Christmas party in two weeks. Have you purchased the gifts yet?" Maddie asked.

"No. Maybe I'll find something cute in Pennsylvania."

"In Pennsylvania? You're not going to buy me something Amish, are you?" Jackie teased. "Because I don't think Erik would be happy if I wore one of those bonnets."

"Maybe. And I believe they call them *kapps*." Candace pursed her lips, then smiled. "Oh, I know. Aren't you dying for one of those boxes where the spider jumps out at you?"

"I have no clue what you're talking about, but that sounds like something Erik might enjoy." She laughed. "You know how he's always pranking everybody at work."

"I'll keep that in mind." Candace tapped her chin.

"Do you have any more events between now and Christmas?" Maddie asked.

"Yes, that one corporate party. It'll be at the country club in Sunnyside."

Maddie sipped her hot tea. "The golf course, right?"

"That's the one."

"But then you're free for the rest of the holidays?" Jackie chugged down the remainder of her drink and wiped her lips with a paper towel.

"Unless something else comes up. I shouldn't have any other weddings between now and Valentine's Day."

"Right. You would have been hired already. It's kind of nice that people plan their weddings so far in advance. It gives you time to prepare." Maddie smiled.

Candace laughed. "*Most* people plan their weddings well in advance, but not everyone. Do you remember the Aames' wedding five years ago? Two weeks. They gave me *two weeks* to pull everything together. To hire a photographer, a baker, a caterer, a florist, a DJ. The most stressful two weeks of my life!"

"Yes, I remember it well. Poor Dad. I can only imagine what he had to deal with." Jackie laughed.

"Poor Dad? Poor me!"

"I hope you charged extra."

"I did. A little."

"Mom! You should have charged a premium with that late of notice," Jackie insisted.

"I felt sorry for the mother of the bride. She was even more stressed out than I was." She shook her head. "Fortunately, they'd already found a venue for the wedding and the reception, had their formal attire, and had sent out their invitations."

"Speaking of invitations, you will be joining us for Christmas breakfast, right? I don't want you spending the holidays alone." Jackie played with her paper towel, then stuffed it into her empty mug.

Candace nodded. "Yeah, I'll be there. Do you want me to bring the French toast breakfast casserole?"

"Definitely! It wouldn't seem like Christmas without it." Maddie's cheerful expression took on a serious, even melancholy look. Candace knew what was coming. "Will you come to the Christmas Eve service this year?"

Candace shook her head. "No, I don't think so."

"You haven't been since Dad died. It's been three years, Mom. Don't you think it's time?" Jackie huffed.

"I'm...not ready."

"You're sure?" Maddie frowned.

"Yes, Maddie, I'm sure." She exhaled an exasperated sigh. After her husband's sudden death, she'd felt like God had abandoned her. She didn't have any plans to step foot into a church anytime soon.

~

Anna lifted baby Mandy over her shoulder and patted her back to relieve her of any excess gas. She smiled when Mary came near and planted herself next to her on the couch. She patted Mandy's back and 'helped' burp the baby.

"Momma, will you teach me how to make a blanket?"

Anna's brow rose. "A blanket? That's a pretty big undertaking."

"I want to make one for Baby Jesus. Mandy's got blankets."

Anna grinned, figuring she meant the 'Jesus' doll in the manger in the nativity scene at the shelter. "Do you want to crochet one or make a quilt?"

She tapped her little chin. "What do you think He'd like better?"

Anna shrugged. "Well, I don't know. I'm sure either one would be fine."

"I wanna make Him a quilt. He'll like all the pretty colors put together."

"In that case, maybe you and *Mammi* can work on it together. You know how she makes beautiful quilts and sells them at Threads of Beauty? I'm sure she'd love to help you."

"She would?" Mary's eyes danced with excitement.

"She's in her sewing room right now. Why don't you go ask her?" Anna lifted her head, meeting Joe's amused expression across the room as he read the latest copy of *The Budget*.

"*Denki*, Momma!" She wrapped her small arms around Anna and planted a kiss on her cheek, then flew from the room. "Christmas is my favoritest time of year!"

FIVE

Candace held her breath, rechecked to make sure her seatbelt was secure, and nudged her small carry-on beneath the seat in front of her. Landings always made her nervous. She glanced out the tiny window as the elements below passed beneath the airplane at unfathomable speeds. She often wondered how the pilots managed to stop the large jets when they seemed to be hurling toward the runway way too fast.

She leaned back against the seat and closed her eyes, thankful when she felt the wheels hit the ground. As the plane slowed, she mentally prepared herself for the weekend's events.

She'd pick up her rental car, then find her hotel. She wouldn't need to contact her clients until tomorrow, so she'd have time to do some shopping.

And hopefully find some answers.

~

Anna set out the last of the baked goods for the day. This venture had proven to be a fruitful one, thanks to Joseph. She never would have imagined the life she had now, just seven years ago when she'd first met Joe and Harv. What an unexpected blessing they'd been in her life!

She couldn't ask for a better husband in Joe. He'd exceeded her wildest dreams. She was so thankful she'd stepped out in faith that fateful day she'd dropped off lunch in the alley. Who would have thought two homeless men could bring such joy to her life? Well, *Der Herr* had known all along.

"Good afternoon," she greeted an *Englisch* woman that walked through the door of the quilt shop.

"Hi. Maybe you can help me? I'm looking for some inexpensive Christmas gifts for my family in California."

"Wow. You came here all the way from California?"

"Yes. I normally don't travel much this time of year, but I have business here this weekend."

"I see." Anna picked up a plate of whoopie pies. "Would you like to try one?"

The woman eyed the plate. "What are they?"

"We call them whoopie pies. It's basically two thin layers of baked cake batter and a frosting-like filling in the middle. We make them in all flavors. These are strawberry."

"Mm...they sound good."

"*Jah*, they are my husband's favorite." She imagined the look on Joe's face when he would discover she'd packed some in his lunch today. "He loves peanut butter and chocolate."

"I can imagine." The woman gingerly took one off the plate and bit into it. "Oh my! This is heavenly." She closed her eyes.

"Here. Take a napkin." Anna smiled. She never tired of seeing customers' reactions to their baked goods. It brought her great satisfaction knowing she could bless them in this way.

"I wish I could buy some of these and take them home with me. Will they be available on Sunday?"

"I'm sorry. We are closed on the Lord's day."

"Of course. Well, maybe I'll swing by Saturday evening then. What time do you close?"

Linda came near and interjected. "Our holiday hours are eight to eight."

"Okay, then. Do I need to make a special order? I'd like a variety. Maybe a dozen, if you can do it."

"*Jah*, a dozen is no problem." Anna smiled.

"Great. Let me look around and then I'll order before I leave."

Anna turned to look at Linda, who beamed. Everyone's spirits always seemed bright this time of year. It was almost as though there were some sort of electric current dancing through the air.

About ten minutes later, the woman brought her purchases to the counter—a pair of faceless Amish dolls, some quilted key chains, and a small lap quilt. "My granddaughter will love these dolls. You don't happen to sell any of those wooden boxes where the spiders jump out, do you?"

Anna looked at Linda, her expression as clueless as her own must be. "No, I don't. Sorry."

"We could ask around for you," Linda suggested.

"That would be great. I'd like to take one home for my son-in-law. He's a prankster and would love something like that."

"We'll let you know when you come back for your whoopie pies. Or you could take one of our cards and give us a call."

The woman reached for a card. "Thank you. I'll do that."

Anna watched as their customer left the store with a smile on her face. The woman had been frowning before she first walked in, like she carried the weight of the world on her shoulders. What a blessing it was to put a smile on someone's face!

She thought about the woman. She seemed awfully familiar. Had she seen her before? *Nee*, probably not. She was from California and she said she'd come for business. It was most likely her first time in the area.

SIX

C andace wiped the tears from her eyes, then clicked off the remote. Why did she insist on watching Hallmark movies every Christmas season? She knew that they always made her cry. Every. Single. Time.

But this one had been worse. It was different than the typical young-beautiful-woman-meets-gorgeous-young-man and they live happily-ever-after. This one had been about a widow who'd lost her husband. Just like she'd lost Jim. But the end resulted in the character finding love again. She didn't think she'd ever be in that position herself. How could she ever replace Jim?

She couldn't.

And finding another good man was just a fairytale anyway. Something that only happened in the movies. Not that she desired another romantic relationship. No, that was the furthest thing from her mind right now.

She nestled between the sheets and thought of her plans for tomorrow. For better or worse, she'd find answers to questions she'd wondered about her entire adult life. After tomorrow, her life would most likely never be the same.

~

Joseph noticed a woman enter the shelter's dining area and walked to meet her. He eyed the woman, most likely in her late forties. By her attire, he guessed her to be some type of social worker or business woman. Certainly not the usual guest to darken the doors of their local homeless shelter. But there was *something*—an uneasiness?—about her that just didn't add up. Was she nervous?

"May I help you, ma'am?"

"Is there a Harvard Worthington here?" She glanced around furtively.

"Not that I know of. It's just me, Harv, and...wait a minute. Harvard? You don't mean Harv, do you?"

"I suppose he *could* go by that name." The woman shrugged. "A shortened version of Harvard."

"Just a minute." Joseph walked into the kitchen in the back and left her standing near the door. "Hey, Harv, is your real name Harvard Worthington?" He nearly snickered, thinking of his friend with such a name.

Harv looked up from the pot of soup he was stirring. "Harvard Worthington?" He chuckled. "Now, there's a name I haven't heard in a long, long time."

"So, it *is* you?"

"Why do you ask, Joe?"

"There's a woman who came to the door. She's asking for a Harvard Worthington."

"Well, ain't that strange?" His lips twisted.

"You want to go see what she wants?"

"Sure, where is she?" Harv glanced over Joe's shoulder, but the doors blocked his view.

"She's standing by the door."

Harv walked to the double doors of the kitchen and looked out one of the long narrow windows. "No, it can't be." His hand covered his heart.

"Who is it?"

"I don't know, but from here she looks an awful lot like my late wife. Virginia."

"She died of cancer, right?"

"Yes. A long time ago." He pointed. "This woman is older than how I remember my Virginia."

"Did she have a sister, maybe?"

Harv shrugged. "I don't know. Don't remember one. But I'm thinking she'd be too young to be her sister."

"Well, why don't you go see who she is? She asked for you."

Harv nodded. "Okay."

"Do you want me to go with you?"

"If you would."

"Sure." Joe smiled.

Side by side, they walked to the door where the woman still patiently stood. "This is my friend, Harv," Joe introduced.

"Are you Harvard Worthington?" She eyed him up and down with a frown.

"Well, officially speaking, yes, pretty lady. But I haven't heard that name in many years."

"Well, it's taken me quite a while to find you. It's not exactly easy to find someone who appeared to have fallen off the face of the earth."

"I guess living on the streets, then with the Amish, will do that to a body." Harv sighed.

"I must say that, with a name like Harvard Worthington, I expected you to live in some fancy manor or something a little more..." she glanced around "...distinguished."

Joe frowned. "I'm sorry, and you are...?"

She dug into her purse and pulled a photo out of her wallet. She handed it to Harvey. "I'm told those are my biological parents. Harvard and Virginia Worthington."

"Your biological..." Harv stared down at a black and white photo of himself and his deceased wife. "I don't understand. We had a little *boy* but he died in infancy."

"When was he born?"

"December, 1968. I was in Nam."

"My birthday is December 10, 1968. John was my twin. I was given up for adoption when I was two."

Harv frowned. "Adoption?"

"I have a letter from my mother—Virginia. She apparently had thought that you died. I did too, because this was all I had to go by. But then when I began looking into my genealogy and searched for a death record, I couldn't find one for you. Only Virginia's."

"Wow. I don't know what to say." Harv looked to Joe and tears misted in his eyes. "Apparently, I have a daughter. I don't know why Virginia would have kept this from me."

"What do you mean? I don't understand. Her letter says that you had passed away. If she thought you were dead, how could she have told you?"

Harv sighed. "I had contact with your mother in the months leading up to her death."

Joe spoke up. "Perhaps she thought it was too late, if the adoption had already gone through."

Harv shrugged. "Perhaps."

"So, what happened that made my mother think you were dead?"

"I didn't return to her after the war in Vietnam. I guess you can say I had to find myself again. I was young and scared and I'd lost faith in myself. I thought your mother would be better off without me. I had no idea we had another little one."

"Would it have made a difference?"

"I'm not sure." Harvey shook his head. "My thinking wasn't right back then. I just figured Virginia could go back to her folks, find some other guy and marry, and live happily ever after. But if I'd known that I had someone else to provide for, my own flesh and blood, it might have been different for all of us. But I didn't trust myself to be a good husband at the time and I didn't think Virginia would want me after the war. So many of our boys came home to disgrace and rejection."

She frowned. "I'm sorry."

Joe interjected, "Excuse me, but I need to get back to the kitchen. Harv, can you handle this?"

~

"Sure, Joe. We wouldn't want these folks to starve." Harvey nodded, then turned to the woman. "What is your name, daughter of mine?"

"My adoptive name is Candace Dixon. But Virginia named me Emily Beatrice, which is evidently after your mother and hers?"

"That's correct. My mother was Emily."

"I always liked it better than Candace."

"Did you have a good life—a good home?"

She smiled and nodded. "The best."

"That's very good to know."

"Mom and Dad weren't perfect, but who is?"

"I certainly ain't."

She glanced down at her phone. "I'm going to be in town for a couple of days. Would you like to join me for lunch?"

"That would be wonderful." He rubbed his forehead. "Where are you staying? You can come out to the farm and stay there. We have an extra room. I know Joe and Anna won't mind."

Joe carried a tray with several bowls and sat them down on the table. "Lunch, you two?"

"Oh, no. I couldn't," Candace said.

"Why not? It's not just for the homeless. It's for whoever the Good Lord brings through our doors. And I know that He *must've* brought you here," Harv insisted.

"You're sure?" Her expression was hesitant.

"Why pay at some fancy rest-au-rant when the Lord has provided a meal for free? Besides, if you feel like you need to contribute, we have a donation box."

"Okay, you've talked me into it." She smiled.

"I hope I'll talk you into staying at the farm too." Harv ingested a spoonful of steaming broth, and nudged Joe.

Joe nodded. "That's right. You're certainly welcome to come and stay. You can join us for supper."

"It's a generous offer, but you all don't know anything about me. How do you know I'm not dangerous?"

Harv winked. "We'll take our chances."

"Harv and I lived on the streets for quite a while. There aren't too many people that surprise us," Joe said. "In fact, that's how my wife and I met."

Candace sputtered and her eyes grew large. "You met your wife on the street?"

"Yep. She brought Harv and me lunch many times." Joe grinned. "I couldn't help but fall in love with her."

"A match made in Heaven," Harvey mused aloud. "Sweet Anna."

"If you'll excuse me." Joe nodded and returned to the kitchen.

"Yep, Joe and Anna have been through a lot."

"I'd love to hear their story sometime."

"Well, I can tell ya. I know they won't be mindin'."

"You're sure?"

"As sure as your mama's in Heaven." Harv smiled, then began his tale. "Miss Anna worked at a quilt shop downtown called Threads of Beauty. It's owned by Miss Linda, she's a great lady too. Anyway, Miss Anna was engaged to a jerk of a guy— Aaron was his name."

"Threads of Beauty? I think I shopped there yesterday."

"Well, what a co-ink-e-dink."

"Wait. Joe's wife was already engaged when they met?"

"Yep. He saved her, for sure. Of course, Joe would say it's the other way around. I guess the Good Lord saved them both."

"So, where does this guy live?"

"Aaron?"

"Yeah."

"He's still there, living in the same district. There was a big ol' fiasco. It's a long story, actually. He tried to frame Joe and it backfired on him. Joe saved him from going to jail by talking the judge into community service."

Candace looked around and surveyed Joe's attire. "Wait. But Joe is Amish? And he lived on the streets?"

"He was shunned at the time."

"Oh."

"Yeah, the district he was originally from was very strict. Joe went against their rules, knowing it would cost him everything."

"So, they just kicked him out onto the streets because he didn't follow the rules?"

"The church would reinstate his membership if he were to go and confess his wrongdoing. But he believed that what he did was the right thing to do. According to the church rules, he could have stayed as a shunned member in his folks' home, but his family didn't want him there. I guess they felt ashamed that he'd gone against the *Ordnung* and was unwilling to confess. So, yeah, he basically was turned away with nowhere to go. All his family was Amish, so it wasn't like he could just move in with a relative."

She shook her head. "Oh, that's so sad. So what did he do?"

"Well, he managed to make his way for a while. Went to school, got a good job, all that."

"What happened then?"

"He became the fall guy for the company he was working for. He basically lost everything he'd worked for, became discouraged, and ended up on the streets. And that's where we met."

"Wow. He's lived a tough life. You'd never guess it by looking at him. He doesn't even seem that old."

"Almost thirty-two." He stared into her eyes. "Everybody has a story. It takes a special person to uncover that story."

"I'd dare say that some don't *want* to tell their stories."

"You're right about that too. Like your mother, Virginia, I suppose." Harv sighed. "We all live with regrets."

"You're absolutely right."

"Oh, how I wish I'd known about you. But then, I guess it would've been too late."

"It's okay. Like I said. I've had a pretty good life." She briefly squeezed his hand. "So, what about you? Did you ever remarry after my mother died?"

"No. I would have made a terrible husband at that time. I'm afraid I drowned my sorrows in alcohol." He shook his head. "But I'm free now. Thanks to Joe and the Good Lord."

"Well, I'm glad to hear that you got your life together."

"And what's your story, daughter of mine?"

She glanced up at the clock on the wall. "I think we'll save that for another day."

"You need to go somewhere?"

"Yeah, I should probably get back to the hotel. I need to contact my client."

"You sure you won't stay with us?"

"No, thank you. I already have reservations. Like I said, I'll only be in town a few days."

"Okay. Is there any way I can talk you into coming for supper?"

"You know, I'd love to. But I have limited time on this trip. I'm actually in town for a wedding, so I'll be really busy." She dug into her purse and pulled out her wallet. She handed him a business card. "You can reach me at this number pretty much anytime. I'll try to keep in touch too."

SEVEN

Harvey watched as his daughter—*his* daughter!—walked out the door. An unanticipated rush of tears flooded his eyes and he swept them away with his fingers. Joe's grip on his shoulder assured him he had a friend who'd support him, no matter what transpired.

"Why don't you take the rest of the day off, Harv? The guys and I can handle it."

"Nah...I'm fine." He straightened.

"I know you, Harv. I'm sure you'll be needing to have a little talk with God. And you'll be wanting to share your news with *Mammi* and Anna too." He pulled the keys to the shelter's van from his pocket and placed them in Harvey's hand. Occasionally, they'd use the van for whenever supplies were running low or someone needed a ride. "Go ahead. I'll catch a ride with one of the guys."

"Appreciate that, Joe."

As Harv drove along the route between the shelter and home, he couldn't suppress the tears that pricked his eyes. He grieved for the life he could have had. If only he'd had the sense to return home after the war. If only he'd had more time with Virginia. If only things had been different.

But dwelling on 'if onlys' wouldn't change his circumstances no matter how much he longed for what might have been. He needed to make right now count. He needed to make wise decisions in the present so he wouldn't regret anything in the future.

Please guide me, Lord.

~

"Joe called," *Mammi* met Harv near the pasture fence, moments after he drove up. "Said you may want to talk."

Harv swallowed, unsure if he could get the words out and maintain dry eyes. "Yep."

She studied his face. "Did something happen?"

He blew out a breath, still not trusting his emotions. He stared out at the horses in the pasture. Hopefully, refocusing his thoughts would keep the tears at bay. "I...apparently, I have a daughter."

Her expression widened. "A *dochder*? *Ach*, that *is* some news."

"I'm still trying to process it. Still trying to get past the fact that Virginia kept it from me. I know I did a lot wrong back then, but..." He shook his head. "To keep a secret of this magnitude..."

Mammi reached over and squeezed his hand. "I'm sure she had her reasons. We cannot go back and change the past, no?"

"I reckon not."

"Then count it as a blessing. Only *Der Herr* knows the whys of these matters. Trust Him."

"She may be coming by some day. Wanted her to come by for supper tonight, but she's not able to make it. I'd like everyone to meet her. Looks a lot like my wife did back in the day."

"We'd love to have her here." She patted the back of his hand.

"I'm just a bit shocked, I guess. I don't know how I'm supposed to feel, what I'm supposed to do." He shrugged, feeling like a lost puppy.

"Just show the love *Der Herr* would show her."

He rambled on. "I'm not even sure where she lives. Didn't even think to ask."

"But you *do* have a way to contact her, *jah*?"

"Yeah. She gave me a card with her number on it."

"I have an idea. Why don't you come up with a list of questions you have for her. That way, when you do see her or talk to her next, you won't forget."

He turned and stared at *Mammi*. "That's a great idea." He shook his head. "I don't even know if she's married or if she has a family. I guess I wasn't thinking too much."

"It wonders me if you weren't *over*thinking." *Mammi* smiled.

"You're right."

"Now that you can focus, you can come up with some questions. Just don't ask them all at once and overwhelm the poor thing."

"No. Wouldn't want to do that. I want her to come back."

"Something tells me that if she made an effort to find you, she's not going to be disappearing too soon. She most likely wants a relationship with her *vatter*."

"You think so?" Harv smiled now. That thought hadn't occurred to him.

"For sure and for certain."

EIGHT

Candace set her cell phone down on the desktop after the client on the other line ended the call. No dinner meeting tonight, which left her free for the evening.

She surveyed her hotel room and sighed, turning on the television. After quickly determining there was nothing on that was worthy of her time, she clicked it off again.

Should she meet up with her biological father or would it be better to just hang out at the hotel? She didn't want to impose, but she *had* been invited...

She thought back to the lunch she'd shared with Harvard Worthington. Wow. He definitely hadn't been what she'd expected, although she was unsure what, or who rather, she was expecting. Maybe someone a little more selfish? Certainly not a voluntary servant.

When she'd pulled up to the homeless shelter, she'd been taken aback. Especially when Harvard had informed her that he'd been homeless himself for a number of years. What must it have been like to have lived on the streets?

Instead of the anger she expected to feel toward him, she felt sorry for him. Sorry that her biological mother had died. Sorry that he'd thought he'd be unloved and unwanted after the war. Sorry he'd never known about her.

But now that he did, could they actually form some sort of father-daughter relationship? She couldn't help but wonder what it would have been like to grow up with Harvard Worthington as her father. Would her presence in his life have kept him off the streets all those years? Or would she have grown up in a dysfunctional home?

One thing was for sure. She couldn't get to know her father by sitting alone in a hotel room. She'd take him up on his offer for dinner. Hopefully, it wouldn't be a mistake.

~

As Candace pulled up to the address, she immediately recognized the white, two-story home as Amish-owned. A stately barn, which most likely housed their buggy horses and other farm animals, stood across the yard from the house. A barren clothesline and a couple of hitching posts marked the distance between the two structures. An empty pasture behind the barn was enclosed by a seemingly unending white fence.

Candace breathed in the fresh country air. Certainly a vast improvement over the California Central Valley. This time of year wasn't too bad air quality-wise for Sanger, but summer was brutal. Especially when the wildfires were running rampant and the smoke settled in the valley. That, combined with smog from the larger outlying cities, made it nearly impossible for someone with allergies or asthma to breathe. She took another breath, savoring its beauty. She could get used to this.

This place is wonderful.

She walked up the porch steps and the door immediately opened at Candace's knock. Her eyes widened. "You're the woman from the quilt shop!"

"And you're Harvey's *dochder*?" The young Amish woman carried a baby on her hip and smiled.

"I am. And you're...?"

"I'm Anna, Anna Bender. Joe's *fraa*. His wife."

"I can't believe this. It's a small world after all!"

Anna's confused expression told Candace she'd probably never heard the Disney theme song.

"Well, it's nice to meet you. Again." Candace smiled. "My name is Candace."

"Won't you come in?" She gestured inside.

"Sure."

Joe sidled up to his wife. "So, you two have already met?"

"*Jah*, she came into Threads of Beauty the other day and bought some of my Amish dolls."

"They're for my granddaughter," Candace explained. "And I ordered some whoopie pies too."

Joe smiled and shared a loving glance with his wife. "They're my favorite!"

Candace laughed. "That's what your wife said."

"Hey, I like 'em too!" Her biological father chimed in.

Joe slapped his back. "Harv, you love every kind of food known to man."

"Well, guess I can't really argue much with ya there." Harvard rubbed his chin. He placed his arm around Candace's shoulder. "What do you say we indulge in some of that delicious food right now, daughter of mine?"

Candace smiled and nodded. "Sounds good."

"Anna? *Mammi*? Is it ready?" Harvard asked.

"*Jah*." Anna replied as she settled one of the little ones at the table.

An older woman spoke up, a potholder in her hand. She pointed at Harvard. "You need to go and wash your hands if you plan on puttin' your feet under my table."

He held up his hands. "These puppies are clean as a whistle."

"And that is the problem." The woman insisted. "Whistles are filthy."

"I suppose I could sit backwards," Harvard teased.

"You won't be gettin' one bite until those hands are scrubbed."

"Yes, *Mammi*." Harvard hung his head in surrender. He gave Candace a fleeting glance, followed by a wink, then slunkered to the bathroom.

Candace hid her amusement. It seemed like Harvard Worthington was a regular stinker.

She wasn't sure what it was, but something delicious wafted through the air, causing her stomach to grumble. Fortunately, no one had noticed but her.

She watched as the women set the food in the middle of the table. "Would you like some help?" She offered.

"Sure," *Mammi* smiled. "You can take that pitcher there and set it on the table."

She did as told.

"Don't forget to save room for dessert. Jacob and Rachel will be joining us later." The older woman said to no one in particular.

"Jacob is Anna's cousin. Moved here about the time me and Joe met Miss Anna and *Mammi*." Harvard winked at the older woman. "*Ain't so?*"

"Those two caused quite a stir," *Mammi* informed Candace.

Candace smiled. "I can imagine."

As soon as everyone was gathered around, the table became silent and Candace noticed each person bowing their heads. She followed their lead. All was quiet for the space of about two minutes, then she heard the sound of tinkling silverware. She looked up and served herself as each item passed. There was chicken, coleslaw, noodles, red beets—she'd passed on those—and fresh bread with apple butter.

Her eyes widened as a pot with thin taupe liquid was passed in front of her.

"Ya ever had coffee soup?" Harvard asked.

She frowned. "Coffee...*soup*?"

"Yep. Dish ya some out into that bowl and put some crackers into it." Harvard suggested. "Mm...mm."

She did as instructed, though unsure if she'd live to regret it.

"Go ahead. Give it a try," her father urged.

She knew her cheeks must be darkening. She couldn't help it while all eyes were on her. She picked up a spoon and took a sip. "Interesting. It tastes like a very mild sweet coffee—with crackers in it." She laughed. "I never imagined coffee and crackers would go together, but somehow it works."

Candace dipped her spoon in again, all the while pondering what other new things she might learn on this adventure. Her trip to Pennsylvania hadn't gone at all like she thought it would—but that wasn't necessarily a bad thing. The people who surrounded her seemed to have a gift of making strangers feel welcome and at home among them. It was a wonderful feeling indeed.

NINE

Candace covertly glanced at the couples that sat around the dessert table and had to stifle the emotion building in her heart. They seemed content—even Joseph and Anna who'd had their share of struggles.

She wanted the closeness she witnessed between Jacob and Rachel, and Joe and Anna—she needed it. Last year had been her third Christmas since Jim passed away. This year would be her fourth Christmas alone. Each year, she hoped that it would get easier—that the void would somehow miraculously be filled, that pain would somehow disappear—but that hadn't been the case.

She and Jim had a good marriage—not perfect—but good. They'd learned to live with each other and had become best friends over the years. Now, she felt lost—like she no longer belonged anywhere. Jim was gone. The children were busy with their own families and had their own lives. Yet, here she was. Stuck in her loneliness. Sure, the children visited. But it was that day-to-day companionship that she missed. Having someone to talk to. To share her hopes and dreams with.

A knock at the door interrupted her self-evaluation.

"Hello, Taylor, come on in." Joseph's voice carried from the other room. "Won't you join us? My wife was just about to serve us some pie and coffee."

"Sure, that'd be great."

Joseph entered the dining area with a good-looking man, most likely a few years older than herself, she surmised. She haphazardly glanced at his hand. He wore a ring, which meant he was already taken.

Taylor spotted her seated at the table. "Oh, I was unaware you had company. I could come back at a different time."

"Oh, no. This is the perfect time," her father spoke up. His grin just as wide as it could be. "Taylor, meet my daughter, Candace."

The man's jaw lowered momentarily, then he recovered with a smile. "I didn't realize Harvey had a daughter." He extended his hand. "It's nice to meet you. I'm a friend of the family."

"Nice to meet you too, Taylor." Candace shook his hand.

Harv clasped the man's shoulder. "Yep. Taylor's our neighbor. He's been coming around much more since he lost his wife last year."

"It's been almost two years ago now," Taylor corrected. "She had cancer." He grimaced.

"Oh, I'm so sorry." Candace frowned.

"Yeah. Not a day goes by that I don't think about her." He shrugged, then placed his hand over his heart. "But my heart is still beating so I know that God must still have a plan for me."

"I completely understand. It's like you still miss them and wished they were here. Sometimes, you wish you could have gone with them. Yet, like you said, you're still here and have to keep on going."

"Have *you* lost someone as well?" He shook his head. "I'm sorry, if that's too personal–"

"No, it's fine. My husband died in a car accident one morning on his way to work about four years ago."

The pain in his countenance told her that he understood. "I'm terribly sorry. It must have been hard for you. To have no warning like that. At least with Diane I knew months in advance that she probably wouldn't be with me much longer. I can only imagine how much more jarring a sudden death would have been."

Candace suddenly surveyed the faces around the table. "Oh, I'm sorry. Here we are just talking away... I didn't mean to monopolize the conversation."

"Oh, no, that's fine," Anna said with a smile of understanding. She and Joseph offered each of them a slice of pie and a steaming mug of coffee. "But if you'd rather talk privately, you're welcome to take your coffee and dessert into the living room and sit by the fire."

"That sounds great." Taylor smiled. "Candace?"

She hesitated, glancing at those seated at the table. "Oh. Well, I wouldn't want to be rude to our hosts."

Harvard spoke up and shooed them away. "Nonsense. You go ahead. We'll have plenty of time to catch up later."

"Okay." She surrendered.

"You first," Taylor insisted she lead the way to the other room.

TEN

Candace placed her drink and dessert on a handcrafted side table and sank into one of the hickory rockers.

Taylor sat in the rocker on the other side of the small table. "It's difficult to talk about Diane sometimes, but I realize it does help relieve some of the pain. It seems worse when I bottle it up inside. I don't want to dishonor her memory by not speaking of her. She was such an important part of my life and I feel like I need to acknowledge that."

"My life felt like it turned upside down the day I lost Jim. Suddenly, I had no clue what to do—how to continue on. In the blink of an eye, I'd lost my best friend, my lover."

He nodded. "That initial shock just stops you in your tracks. All of a sudden, every little distraction that seemed so important before, now it didn't even matter. Nothing mattered. Except breathing and waking up the next morning to another grueling lonely day."

"Oh, man. Exactly. That's precisely how I've felt."

"You just have to take that time and grieve. But it's important to remember your loved ones. I think of our children, and I know that Diane wouldn't want me to neglect my relationship with them."

"How many children do you have?"

"Two." He smiled.

"Me too. They both have families of their own now."

"I have one married and one plugging his way through college."

"What do you do for a living?"

"I'm a real estate agent. You?" He took a sip of his coffee.

"I'm an event planner. I mostly do weddings."

Taylor dug into his pie and groaned. "Oh, man, this is delicious. *Mammi* makes the best pies."

She forked a bite into her mouth as well. The buttery crust practically melted in her mouth. "You're right. This is heavenly."

"So, weddings, huh? That sounds interesting. Weekends are a busy time for you then, I'm assuming?"

"Very."

"Do you attend church anywhere?"

Candace shook her head. "Not regularly. Not anymore." Her brow rose. "Do you?"

"Oh, yes. I don't know how I would have gotten over Diane's death without my church family. They really helped with encouragement. I guess you can say, other than that, church keeps me busy and helps to occupy my mind." He blew out a breath. "That's why I help out at the shelter every now and then and why I'm here now. I've really come to enjoy everyone's company here. Being surrounded by friends helps immensely."

"I don't know. It seems like church works for some people. Not so much for others."

"What do you mean?"

She shrugged. "Well, Jim was certainly more spiritual than me. He was the one who enjoyed church—wanted to go almost every week. When he passed, I just didn't really see a reason to keep going."

Taylor frowned. "Do you think this is what he would want you to do?"

"No, he'd probably be disappointed." She sighed. "Church never was my strong point."

He smiled. "Do you know the purpose of church?"

"No, not really. It seems to me like a place where people go to show off their new outfits and pretend they're better than everybody else."

"Hmm...I've always thought of church as a place to spend time with friends and a hospital for spiritually wounded people."

She glanced at the crackling fire. "Really?"

"Yeah. I just know that each time I attend a service, I feel like a burden has been lifted off my shoulders. It gives me a spiritual vitamin shot, if you will."

"Well, maybe I've just gone to the wrong church."

He shrugged. "Could be. You're welcome to attend services at my church."

"I might just take you up on that offer." Although she had no idea when she'd find time. Perhaps this Sunday? She needed to be back in Sanger by the end of next week to watch the grandchildren.

He smiled and Candace noticed easy laugh lines around his eyes. "I'd like that."

I'd like that. Taylor's words played over in her mind. He wanted her to attend his church.

"I could pick you up and we could ride together."

"Oh." She was taken aback. "Really?"

"Sure. I'd be happy for the company."

"I need to tell you that I actually live in California, so this will probably be just a one-time deal. I'm only here for a couple of days."

"Whoa, California?" Disappointment creased his brow. "You're a long way from home. What brought you out here?"

"A wedding, actually. Looking up my father was something I wasn't sure I would have the nerve to do." She smiled.

"Yet, here you are."

"Yep, here I am. Before today, everyone in this house had been a stranger to me."

"Imagine that." He frowned. "So, you'd never met Harvey before today?"

She shook her head. "No. I thought he was deceased. I was adopted as a toddler and only recently began researching my genealogy. When I couldn't find a death record for my biological father, I figured there was a good chance he was still alive."

"Wow, that's...amazing."

"It is, isn't it? To think I still have a living parent."

"What about your adoptive parents?"

"They were both older when they adopted me, so it was almost like growing up with grandparents. They've both passed on."

"That's too bad."

"Yeah, but it's beyond my control. Like everything else in this life, it seems." She shrugged. "I also discovered that I'd had a twin brother who died as a baby. Which explained why I experienced a lot of loneliness growing up."

"Makes sense." He nodded. "So, Harvey must've been pretty excited to see you after all these years, huh?"

"That's another thing that's extraordinary. He never knew I existed. Apparently, he was off at war and my mother never told him about me. Of course, she'd assumed he was dead when she gave me up for adoption, so it wasn't really her fault. She had cancer and learned she'd die soon."

"That's tragic."

"It is." She dug into her purse and handed him a photo. "This is all I had of my biological parents."

"Wow, you look a lot like your mother." He chuckled. "And look at Harvey. He was a handsome fellow."

"Yes, it seems like they made a good couple."

"I've drained my coffee. I think I'll get another cup." Taylor stood. "Would you like to join the others now? I'd hate to prevent you from spending time with your father, especially since the two of you just met."

Candace smiled. "Sure."

"Hey." He briefly touched her shoulder. "Thank you for sharing your story with me."

Candace nodded, an inexplicable warmth filling her heart, then led the way back into the dining area.

~

Candace practically fell into her bed at the hotel the moment she arrived. What an evening!

Tomorrow she'd be occupied with the wedding all day. She'd agreed to attend church with Taylor on Sunday morning. And then...what? Her flight was scheduled to leave Monday morning, but she wasn't ready to return home yet. She hadn't spent enough time getting to know her new-found family and friends.

She snapped her fingers. Her mind was made up. She'd call the airline tomorrow and postpone her flight a few days. That would give her extra time with her family, yet she'd still make it in time to babysit for Jackie on Friday.

It was a once-in-a-lifetime opportunity, so why not?

ELEVEN

Taylor pulled into the hotel parking lot and picked up his cell phone to text Candace.

I'm in the parking lot. Dark blue Explorer.

He blew out a breath and fidgeted with his tie. Maybe he should have left the thing at home. He didn't always wear ties, but when he did, he usually wished he didn't. He pulled the thing away from his neck and tried to straighten it in his mirror. It was just so hard to get the things to cooperate.

His phone dinged and he read Candace's reply.

Be down in a minute.

He kept an eye on the hotel entrance and, sure enough, Candace strolled out a moment later. He stepped out of his car and waved to get her attention. She spotted him and headed over, an attractive smile on her face.

"Good morning!"

"Good morning," he returned, opening the passenger door for her.

She took a seat. "Thank you."

He shut her door then quickly moved to his side and hopped in. "Did you sleep well?"

"I did, thank you. I was pretty exhausted after the wedding last night. The reception lasted a good three hours."

"Oh, how did that go?"

"It was great! Such a beautiful ceremony. I never tire of seeing two people commit the rest of their lives to each other."

Taylor smiled, remembering when he had done just that. Nearly twenty-five years ago.

"You know, I'd never thought about it before, but God is the Ultimate Wedding Planner." He grinned.

"What do you mean?"

"Well, the church—God's people—are called the bride of Christ. When Jesus was on earth, He said He was going to prepare a place for His bride. And one of the first events on the heavenly timetable is the wedding supper of the Lamb."

He eyed her clueless expression. "I'm sorry. Did all that just go over your head?"

She laughed. "Pretty much."

"I'm sorry. I tend to get carried away sometimes." He chuckled. "Do you ever do that? Think you have this great idea and you explain it to other people and nobody gets it?"

74

She laughed again. "Can't say I do."

"There I go again." He shook his head and chuckled. "I guess I'll just shut up now."

Silence reigned for half a minute until Candace spoke. "So, your church..."

"What about it?"

"Any tips? Warnings? Comments?"

He laughed and glanced over at her, noticing how tense she seemed. "Are you nervous?"

"A little."

"Don't be. You'll be fine." Taylor reached over and touched her clenched hand. Her gaze flew to his and he pulled back, sending her a reassuring smile. "As far as warnings though, there is Buddy. He's an older man that attends church. He loves to hug people. Even if you're just visiting. He greets everyone the same way. So be prepared for that."

"That's sweet."

"He's a great guy. And my only comment regarding church is this: Open your heart to whatever God has to show you."

~

Candace quietly eyed Taylor over the rim of her glass of lemon water. She liked this guy. Really liked him.

Their morning at his church had gone surprisingly well and she'd been shocked at just how much she enjoyed herself. The different, but welcoming, congregation had brought new life to her soul and being around Taylor seemed to be healing her heart.

She couldn't put her finger on exactly why she was so attracted to him. Perhaps it was his handsome features or the way his easy-going, steadfast manner reminded her of her husband, Jim.

Taylor glanced up and met her gaze and she refrained from looking away. She lowered her glass. "I had a really good time at your church."

His lips curved in a smile. "Despite getting crushed by Buddy?"

"Yes. Although you could have warned me he had such a strong grip. I wasn't expecting a bear hug."

Taylor laughed and Candace realized just how much she loved that sound.

"Sorry."

She smiled. "It's okay. I really enjoyed it all, Buddy included."

"I'm glad to hear it."

"It wasn't quite like I was expecting."

"How so?"

"Everyone was so... genuine. I really appreciated that. I'm used to everyone putting on a charade. Your church was different."

"I'm glad you thought that. How I see it, there's no charade to put on. Everyone goes through life and faces their trials and triumphs, whether they try to hide it or not. It's better to keep things real."

"I agree."

Their waitress approached and took their orders, then left with the menus.

Candace spoke up. "Thank you, again, for bringing me here. You really didn't have to."

"It's no problem. It's only fair that I treat you to lunch after bringing you to church. Southern hospitality and all." He emphasized the drawl.

"Oh, I didn't realize you were from the South." She settled her chin onto her palm.

"Tennessee, actually. Not the deep South, but the whole good manners aspect has a far reach." He winked and she found herself grinning.

"I see."

"My family and I moved out here about fifteen years ago, but before that, I'd never lived outside of the state."

"Do you miss it?"

"Not really. The landscape and weather here are pretty similar to Tennessee. I do miss my brother and sister and their families though. We unfortunately don't get to see each other as much as we used to. My in-laws as well. We're pretty close."

"That's great. My mother and father-in-law have both passed on."

"Oh. That's unfortunate."

"It is. And it was difficult for my children, of course, losing their grandparents. And then their father."

"Difficult for you as well, I can imagine." Taylor's perceptive gaze probed hers.

She remembered the lonely nights she spent mourning all she had lost and struggled to keep the tears from surfacing. "Very." She blinked hard. "But I've managed."

Taylor nodded. "Only by God's grace."

A hesitant smile broached her lips at his comment, but she remained silent, unsure of what to say to that.

"It's something my son reminded me of just after Diane, my wife, passed. It was one of those moments when you hear something that is completely out of character and there is no doubt in your mind that it was the Lord working through that individual."

"What do you mean?"

Taylor smiled and looked down at his plate, seeming to step back in time as he explained. "It was the day after Diane's funeral and Jarett, our son who was a senior in high school at the time, had been silent all day. All week, in fact. I hadn't heard him speak more than a handful of words since his mother died.

"Anyway, I was sitting on the couch, staring at a photo of Diane, just in a daze. I was barely able to process my surroundings and I hadn't even noticed Jarett was there until he walked up to me and knelt on the floor in front of the couch. He set his hand on my knee and said, 'Dad, we will get through this. Only by God's grace will we get through this.'"

Taylor lifted his gaze to hers, his eyes wet with tears. "There is no doubt in my mind that God was speaking through my son. And he was right. With time, and by God's grace, we have made it through."

"Wow." Candace picked up her napkin and used it as a tissue to wipe her eyes. "That's incredible."

He nodded. "I've seen God do some pretty incredible things."

"I wish I had your faith."

His serious eyes met hers. "You can, Candace. You can have that faith in your life."

"I know. I just... I'm not sure that I'm ready."

Their waitress approached with their food. After she left, Candace turned to Taylor. "Maybe we can continue this conversation later?"

He sent her a gentle smile. "Okay."

TWELVE

"So you're sure Fisher's Furniture has the jumping-spider box?" Candace's gaze flew from the scenery zooming by to Taylor.

He nodded, tapping a finger on the steering wheel. "Positive. I distinctly remember because Jonathan, he's the owner, scared me half to death with one."

Candace chuckled. "Are you afraid of spiders?"

"Not especially, but I was completely unprepared for the thing to jump out at me. I'd just gone into the store for the first time, looking for a nightstand. Jonathan and I had been talking for probably two minutes when he said there was something he had to show me and gave me the box." He shook his head. "I'm surprised he hasn't lost customers because of that thing. Maybe he usually waits until after they buy what they want before springing it on them."

She grinned. "Or maybe you were just the one lucky customer."

"I think you mean unlucky."

"Tomato, to*mah*to."

Taylor laughed and they settled into a comfortable silence as he drove down the highway toward Paradise, Pennsylvania. Candace watched him from the corner of her gaze as he studied the road. He'd been rather happy, she thought, when she let him know that she was staying until Thursday. And when he had heard about her quest for a jumping-spider box, he had immediately told her about Fisher's and offered to take her there. An hour's drive with just the two of them.

It seemed her interest in him was reciprocated, something that both excited her and scared her at the same time. Who would have thought a search for her father would result in her meeting a wonderful man? Certainly not her.

She hadn't even allowed herself to consider having a romantic relationship with anyone after her husband passed away. It was difficult to imagine anyone other than Jim filling that void. On the other hand, it was definitely a void. She felt it every waking moment, the chasm beside her. The idea that that empty space could once again be filled was both amazing and frightening to consider.

"So you're wanting the spider box for your son-in-law?" Taylor's voice broke into her thoughts.

"Yes. Erik. He loves pulling pranks on people. He's a real jokester."

"How long have he and your daughter been together?"

"About eight years. They've been married for seven and have three children."

"That's great. I'm looking forward to grandchildren, whenever the Lord decides to bless me with some."

"Isn't your daughter married?"

"Yes. She got married just last year. No little ones yet though."

"I'm sure it'll happen someday."

"I hope so. For now, I'm just trying to be patient. And I've sort of claimed Mary, Little Joe, and Mandy as my step-grandchildren with how often I've visited Joe and Anna and occasionally helped out at the shelter with Joe and Harv."

"Oh yes, I was able to meet Mary the other night. She's so sweet and I can already tell she has a giving heart. The moment I said hello to her, she asked me what I thought she should give to Baby Jesus as a Christmas present." She looked at him. "What do you even say to that?"

Taylor shook his head. "That's a difficult one, for sure."

"Tell me about it." Candace sighed. "My younger daughter, Maddie, was like that as a little girl, always asking questions that seemed way too wise to have come from a child and were hard for me to answer. She was very curious and always had something to say."

"A child's mind is an amazing thing."

"Indeed."

They again settled into companionable silence and Candace divided her time between enjoying the scenery out her window and stealthily watching Taylor. Before long, they reached Paradise and soon located Fisher's Furniture.

"This is it," Taylor announced, applying the parking brake.

Candace clicked off her seatbelt and sent him a grin. "Let's go check it out."

They exited the vehicle and entered the shop.

"*Guten morgen,* Taylor! How *gut* to see you." An Amish man, who appeared to be slightly older than the two of them, approached. By the always-up-to-no-good look on his face, Candace assumed this was Jonathan Fisher, the store's proprietor.

Taylor shook the man's hand. "Good to see you too, Jonathan. Or should I say Minister Fisher?"

He waved a hand in front of his face. "Just Jonathan. Minister Fisher is for Sundays." He turned to Candace. "Who's your friend?"

"This is Candace. Candace, meet Jonathan."

"Hello." She smiled, imagining the possibility of Jonathan and her father being good friends.

"Candace is in search of a Christmas present."

Jonathan's face lit up. "I have the perfect thing!" He scurried off and returned a few seconds later holding a small box Candace assumed was home to a jumping spider. He handed it to her, a mischievous twinkle in his eye.

Candace faked confusion and studied the box. "What is it?"

"Just open it and see." Jonathan was practically rocking on the balls of his feet in anticipation of her reaction.

She took hold of the little knob on top of the box and slid open the flap, using every ounce of self-control she could muster to not flinch when the spider leapt out on her hand. She looked up at Jonathan and shrugged. "It's cute."

Jonathan's mouth dropped open. "That's it?" He turned from her to Taylor. "It didn't scare you at all?"

He looked so disappointed Candace couldn't help but laugh out loud. Taylor joined in and Jonathan eyed them both suspiciously.

Candace wiped the moisture from her eyes. "That's what I came here to find. A spider box for my son-in-law."

"I warned her that you might try to scare her like you did me." Taylor smirked.

Jonathan grinned at Candace. "Did he tell you that it scared him so much that he fell backwards?"

Candace laughed and looked at Taylor, whose cheeks reddened. "Really?"

Taylor nodded. "I tripped."

"Never seen a grown man so scared," Jonathan added.

"Alright, alright, that's enough about me. I think Candace was wanting to...look around?"

She took pity on Taylor and let him change the subject. "Yes, I'd like to see what else you have. And I definitely want a spider box."

THIRTEEN

Candace was so thankful she'd taken a few extra days to stay and get to know her wonderful new family. She was almost saddened that her time here was coming to an end, though she did miss her grandchildren back home.

"I can't wait till Christmas! It's my favoritest time of year." Mary beamed as she traipsed into the room, carrying a faceless doll with her.

"Why? What do you like about it?"

Mary climbed up onto the sofa and sat next to Candace. She took the time to make sure her doll was properly seated as well, even moving the doll's skirt to cover her legs. "Because we get to have a birthday party for Jesus. I 'specially like all the lights."

"But you're Amish. You don't have lights, do you?"

"Yep. I got the lights inside my heart. *Dat* says that's all we need. But it's fun to see the *Englischers* put lights up on the outside of their fancy houses. Because Jesus is the Light of the World."

"He is, huh?"

"Yep. He lights the way to Heaven."

Candace pondered Mary's words. How could this little girl be so sure about her faith?

~

Candace sipped her coffee. The restaurant's crackling fire reminded her again that Christmas was just around the corner. It would be nice if some of the eastern weather could make its way out west. What would it be like to have more than a quarter inch of snow in Sanger? Not that they even got that. But they had one or two years. It would be laughable to these Easterners, she was sure.

"You look deep in thought. What's on your mind?" Taylor's voice interrupted her musings.

It would be the last evening they'd spend together and the last with her new-found family. A part of her wished it would never end.

"I was thinking about Christmas, and a conversation I had with Mary earlier today. She has such faith. There are no doubts in her mind, whatsoever. Sometimes I wish I could have that kind of assurance."

"Well, Jesus said that we must have faith as a little child. Mary is a classic example of this. Children believe what they hear. Their minds haven't been tainted by the lies of the world. You know, believing in God is something that is instinctual, I think.

It's like God puts a longing inside each human being, and that longing can only be filled by Him. If we never fill that longing, our lives will always feel like they are missing something. There will always be a certain emptiness inside."

Candace pondered his words. It was almost like they were directly for her, like God had put them in his mouth. Hadn't she felt like something was missing? She'd never embraced Jim's faith. There had always been something that held her back. Most likely all the unanswered questions she'd had. But now that her questions were being answered, could she continue to use that as an excuse?

~

Candace turned to Taylor as he pulled into the hotel parking lot. His face was illuminated by the lights along the outside of the building.

"Thanks for dinner and everything. I had a really great time."

He smiled. "I've enjoyed getting to know you. I hope we don't lose contact after you return to California."

"We won't. I have your number, you have mine. We'll keep in touch."

"We can video chat too, if you'd like. And I'd be more than willing to help you stay connected with your father and Joe and Anna. Maybe go over there once in a while so you can chat with them?"

"Oh, I would love that! I was wondering how that would go, since Harvard doesn't own a cell phone." Candace reached across the center console and gave Taylor a brief hug. "Thank you."

"It's been my pleasure, Candace. Truly." He set his hand on top of hers and her pulse quickened. Taylor leaned forward, his gaze shifting from her eyes to her lips and back again in an unspoken question.

How long had it been since she had kissed a man? Not that she really needed to ask herself. She knew exactly when—the day Jim had died. How wonderful it would be to have him back. To hold him in her arms and kiss him again. To fall asleep with him at her side.

Candace quickly pulled away from Taylor before she did something foolish. How had he become Jim in her mind? In that moment, she had wanted to wrap him in her arms and never let go. She pictured Jim, not Taylor. But Jim was gone. And never coming back again.

Taylor hesitantly reached for her hand. "Candace? Is everything alright?"

Candace shook her head. She braced herself on the car door. "No. This can't happen. We can't...it just...it can't happen."

A furrow appeared in Taylor's forehead. "Why not?"

"I don't think I can do this, Taylor. You're a wonderful man, you are. It's just...well...I live in California and you live here. I'm about to go back home and where does that leave us? I don't want to lose another man I care about. I'm sorry. I have to go." She quickly opened the door and got out of his car before he could reply. "Goodbye, Taylor."

She grabbed her things and shut the door, hoping to reach her hotel room before allowing her tears to fall.

FOURTEEN

Candace's eyes roamed the room, taking in the Christmas decorations in her daughter's home. Lights twinkled on the fresh fir tree, presents were stacked beneath it, a 'Jesus is the Reason for the Season' plaque hung on the wall, a nativity scene graced the top of the bookshelf. Christmas morning had to be one of her favorite days of the year.

As Candace sat at the table with her loved ones gathered around, she couldn't help but wonder what her other family was doing. Her Amish family. Well, her father wasn't *exactly* Amish but he lived with the Amish and considered them family right now. Which meant she could call them family too.

She hadn't missed the spark between him and *Mammi* either. She wondered if their relationship went beyond the simple friendship they wanted everyone to believe they had. To her, they seemed like a good match.

Did she *want* her father to have a relationship with another woman? Not that it was any of her business. Harvard Worthington could marry whomever he wanted. And since her biological mother had been deceased for nearly five decades, who was she to begrudge him a life companion?

Her thoughts wandered to Taylor. He really was an amazing man of great faith. How could he be doing so well when his wife had only passed on less than two years ago? The thought boggled her mind.

Had it already been three weeks since they'd seen each other? She had to admit that she missed him. And her new family.

It had been kind of Taylor to call to see if she'd made it home all right. He was a wonderful friend. She'd been surprised how quickly and how well they'd clicked. As though they'd been old friends. It wasn't that she didn't have any interest in exploring their relationship to see if it led to more. She pretty much saw where it had been leading. She was almost certain Taylor was about to kiss her. But what could ever become of it?

She shook her head.

"Mom?"

Candace's head snapped up. What had she missed?

"Did you even hear a word of what we said?" Jackie sounded exasperated.

"Can't say I did. Sorry." She really should be enjoying her family's presence instead of pondering what would never be.

"You've been acting strange ever since you returned from Pennsylvania. What's up?"

She blew out a breath. "Well, I guess since everyone is here, I might as well share the news."

"News?" All eyes turned to her.

"Yeah. You know how I've been researching my genealogy, right?"

They nodded.

"Well, I'd thought that all my older family members had passed on. But I never found a death certificate for my biological father." She took another deep breath. "The last trace of him led to Pennsylvania, not far from the wedding I'd coordinated."

"And?"

"I'm getting to it." She smiled. "It's a long story. I found him at a homeless shelter."

"Wait. Your biological father is homeless?" Jackie asked.

She shook her head. "No. But he used to be. He was just there helping out."

"So, what did he say?" Maddie smiled.

"He had no clue that I existed."

"What? Really? How?" Jackie's confused expression reminded Candace of herself when she'd made the discovery.

"Well, he and my mother were separated for several years when he was in the Vietnam War and after he returned. When he discovered she was sick, that's when they reconnected again. That was just a couple months before she passed on. She'd originally assumed my father was dead and knew she wasn't going to be there to take care of me, so she gave me up. When my mother and father finally reconnected, she never told him about me. I'm guessing because she'd already given me up for adoption and there was no way he could get me back?" She shrugged.

"Or maybe she didn't tell him because she didn't want to disrupt your life?"

"Could've been. Whatever it was, she had her reasons. But my biological father had known about my twin brother John that died as an infant. Virginia, my mother, didn't tell him about me at the time for whatever reason."

"Oh, wow. That's sad." Maddie's husband chimed in.

Candace nodded.

Maddie's eyes grew large. "So, how did he react? I bet he was shocked."

"Yeah, pretty much."

"So, we have another grandpa then?" One of her grandchildren brightened.

Candace smiled. "A great grandpa."

"What sort of a person is he?" Jackie asked.

"He's kind, cares about others." Candace looked at Erik. "He's funny and a little silly. Kind of reminds me of you, Erik."

"When do we get to meet him?" Erik rubbed his hands together.

"Well, he's in Pennsylvania. He's older, so I don't know how he'd feel about traveling all the way across the U.S."

"Couldn't we go see him? Maybe get a train fare when the tickets are cheap?" Maddie looked hopefully at her husband Brad.

"That's an idea." Candace nodded.

Jackie frowned. "So, did he ever remarry?"

"No. But he lives with an Amish family. I think he might have a crush on the older woman that lives there."

"Amish? How did *that* happen?" Maddie asked.

"That's an even *longer* story. How about if we talk about it later? I wouldn't want to keep these kiddos from opening up their presents!"

As the table was cleared and the children opened their gifts, Candace couldn't help but wonder how her family in Pennsylvania celebrated Christmas. She couldn't recall any decorations.

They didn't have electricity, so there were no twinkling lights anywhere. Although she imagined the glow of a lantern's dancing flame had an appeal all its own.

Did they put up a tree? Decorate the house? Give gifts to each other?

As Candace mused, her son-in-law's laugh soon distracted her. "This is perfect! Hey, Brad, check this out!"

FIFTEEN

Harv welcomed Taylor into the house, excited to be able to communicate with his daughter. Taylor stomped the snow off his boots.

"The snow finally arrived, eh?" Harv shivered. "Glad I ain't out in that anymore! Thanks to my sweet angels."

Taylor's brow rose. "Angels?"

"Yep. Miss Anna, *Mammi*, and Miss Linda."

Joe came to the entryway and shook Taylor's hand. He glanced at Harv. "Hey, what about me?"

"What about you? You were as hopeless as I was." Harv grinned.

"Maybe so, but I was the one who hooked us up with this gig." Joe opened his arms and turned a half circle.

Harv howled in laughter. "What, you been hangin' out with rappers now? And you know good and well that it was the Good Lord Who 'hooked us up with this gig.'" He chuckled again.

"No rappers. I work at the shelter, remember?"

"Say no more."

Taylor shook his head and laughed. "You two."

"Can't wait to see that daughter of mine again." Harv smiled. "Whatcha got there, Taylor?"

"I brought my tablet this time. Thought it would be easier to see everyone with a larger screen."

"Good idea." Joe nodded. "I'll call everyone into the living room."

Taylor dialed the number, then set the tablet up with its cover's stand-up feature. "Hey, Candace. Your family's here!"

"Hi, everyone! I've missed you all. Are you enjoying your winter weather?"

~

Joe finished brushing down Brazen, then set the brush back on the hook where it belonged. He surveyed the barn, making sure everything was in order before he returned to the house. And hopefully to some of Anna's whoopie pies.

The chilly early March air told him another snowstorm was approaching with a vengeance.

The telephone's shrill ring pierced the air and he picked it up. He didn't want to offer a greeting lest it be one of those people trying to sell something. They always waited for you to speak first, then they'd begin their sales spiel.

He nearly hung up when Harv's hearty voice called through the phone line. "Hello, pretty lady!"

Joseph chucked. "I've been called a lot of things before, Harv, but *that* was not one of them. Until now."

"Joe!" He sputtered. "I didn't know you'd be home. Thought you was working."

"I was, but I came home early. Heard we were supposed to get some snow and I didn't want to be stuck out there in it. Where are you?"

"Stuck out here in it."

"Oh, no. You at the shelter?"

"Yeah. I'm just thinkin' of hunkerin' down here for the night."

"You sure? I can call Taylor and ask him to come pick you up."

"Nah, I'll be fine. Not the first time sleeping in a shelter, you know." Harv chuckled.

"Oh, I know all too well. How could I forget? Let's just not make a habit of it, alright?"

"Alright."

"And Harv?"

"What is it, Joe?"

"Don't go eating all the food."

A loud gasp echoed through the line. "What? *Me*?"

Joe grinned. "And don't do anything foolish, like try to walk home in a blizzard. I don't feel like calling out a search party to go looking for you."

"What are you, Joe? My mother?"

"Sometimes it feels like it, Harv. Sometimes it feels like it."

"Well, don't you go worryin' about me none. You just look after your own."

"Harv, you *are* one of my own."

"Yeah, yeah. Just let *Mammi* know so she don't worry about me."

"Okay, will do. Stay warm." Joe clicked off the phone and offered a silent prayer for his buddy.

No, Harv wasn't blood related, but Joe couldn't help but feel like kin to him. He and Harv had been through a lot together. He didn't even want to think of the day when Harv would be gone from his life.

He wouldn't think about it.

SIXTEEN

Taylor tapped his trousers, hoping he hadn't made a mistake in coming. Would Candace like his surprise? Would he be bothering her? He hated to think of the latter.

Fortunately, her daughter Jackie had informed him that her mother had the week free. He'd been communicating with Candace's daughter via private social media messages and he'd been able to get some great advice from her.

He wiped the sweat from his brow. Whew, was it a hot day! Were Julys always this bad in the California Central Valley? The temperature gage in his rental car had shown one hundred and ten degrees. He figured it had to be wrong, but standing out here in it now felt like the reading could have been accurate. He could probably guzzle a gallon of water right about now. Hopefully, Candace would allow him entry before he melted away.

He held the bouquet of flowers in front of him. A dozen red roses wasn't too much, was it? She already knew that he cared for her—he'd made that clear. He was certain that she just needed time to figure out what she wanted. He promised himself, though, that he wouldn't allow anything serious until she became a believer. As much as he cared for Candace, he couldn't pursue a serious romantic relationship with someone he'd be unequally yoked to. He'd have to walk carefully where Candace was concerned. Perhaps he should have purchased yellow flowers instead?

After a moment, the door opened, accompanied by a gasp. "Taylor!" Candace's hand immediately went to her damp hair. She must've just had a shower.

Thankfully, a blast of cool air hit him. Air conditioning *had to* be a gift from God.

Apparently, he'd caught her off-guard. "I'm sorry if I found you at a bad time." He grimaced.

"No, I... Wow, I can't believe you're *here*. On *my* doorstep! Won't you come in?"

"Gladly." He handed her the bouquet. "These are for you."

"Thank you. That's very kind."

"Your daughter said you had the week off, so..."

"Jackie! I'm gonna kill her." She shook her head. "Look at me. I'm a mess."

"Most beautiful mess I've ever seen." Taylor smiled. "Don't blame your daughter. It's my fault. I wanted to surprise you for your birthday."

"Well, you've definitely succeeded."

His excitement deflated. "I'm sorry. I could go and come back at a more convenient time."

"Oh, no. Don't think that I don't want you here. It's just...a woman usually wants to look her best when..." Her hand brushed through her hair. "Oh my, I have made a mess of this. Will you go back outside so I can answer the door again?"

"In that heat?" He teased.

"It *is* hot, isn't it?" She shook her head. "Would you like something to drink? I have tea and water."

"Water would be great."

"Okay. By the way..." She smiled and embraced him. "Thank you for coming."

"My pleasure." He briefly held her tight—it felt good to have her in his arms—then released her. He needed to tread lightly, he reminded himself. They were just friends.

"I'm going to put these beautiful roses into a vase and get that water for you."

He watched her walk into the open kitchen. "Sure."

"Feel free to take a seat in the living room," she called over her shoulder, pulling out a glass vase from one of the overhead kitchen cupboards. She took a water bottle out of the refrigerator and handed it to him. "I'm just going to go freshen up a minute. You don't mind, do you?"

"No, of course, not. Go ahead and do whatever you need to do." He unscrewed the cap and took a swig of the water. "Don't worry about me. I'll just hang out here."

"Go ahead and look around, if you'd like." Her voice echoed from down the hall.

"Okay." He'd been so nervous when he first walked in, he hadn't even realized he'd entered through a foyer. An elegant side table, where she'd placed his bouquet of flowers, graced the entrance. The vaulted ceilings added a nice touch, and accented the home's tasteful décor. He'd always preferred earth tones over bold colors. Candace's home was attractive, and tidy considering she hadn't been expecting company. The smell of citrus lured his gaze to an essential oil diffuser, something he'd recently learned about from his daughter. All in all, the home had an open airy feeling about it. It was quite pleasant.

Taylor sighed and eventually took a seat. He eyed a photo on the wall of Candace and her deceased husband. He stood and moved to take a closer look. The wedding photo showed the happy couple standing at the top of church steps.

"Jim and I were so young there." Candace said from behind him.

"How old were you?"

"Twenty. He was twenty-three."

"That *is* young." He pointed to the photo. "You both look very happy."

"We were, although we were also inexperienced and unprepared for the struggles of married life."

"I don't know if one can ever adequately prepare for something like that. Kind of like having children. You just learn as you go." He returned to the overstuffed couch and sat down.

Candace sat near the opposite end. "So, you came all this way to surprise me?"

He nodded. "I've missed you. I wanted to do something special for your birthday."

Her smile broadened. "That's really sweet. How long will you be in town for?"

He finished the last of his water. "Just a couple of days."

"Where did you have in mind to take me?"

"I wanted it to be a surprise, but your daughter said that it's quite a bit of a drive and you'd figure it out anyway." He shrugged.

"Might as well spill the jelly beans."

"Jelly beans, huh? That's cute." He grinned. "I have it on good authority that you enjoy dining at Medieval Times. I guess it's in the LA vicinity?"

She gasped. "Really? You're going to take me all the way to Medieval Times?"

"I was hoping to visit one of the beaches out that way too. I've never seen the Pacific."

"Oh, it sounds wonderful!"

He reached for her hand. "I hope it will be."

SEVENTEEN

Candace yawned. She wasn't used to getting up at five in the morning. She peeked over at Taylor, who looked every part the commandant of his SUV. He was most likely a morning person. She, on the other hand, was not. It had been the same with her and Jim.

"I thought we could stop for breakfast somewhere along the way." He glanced her direction.

"That sounds good. We can eat at the bottom of the Grapevine, if you'd like."

His lips twisted. "Grapevine?"

"It's a stretch of highway, between the valley and LA, that winds through the mountains."

"Oh, so we'll actually get to see more than desert and field after field of produce? Although, I do admit that it's fascinating. The topography is so different in this part of the country. Everything is flat and straight."

"I know. Not too much greenery unless you climb to the higher elevations. The state of California is actually pretty diverse, as far as topography is concerned. This is just the valley."

"When I drove into town and first saw the sign for 'Sanger— The Nation's Christmas Tree City,' I admit that I expected more trees."

"Oh, that's in reference to Sequoia National Park. Some of the largest trees in the world are there. They're pretty impressive."

His brow rose. "Really?"

"Yeah. Too bad you won't be around longer. I'd take you up there. It's not that far." She smiled. "That's one thing that I like about living where I do. I'm about an hour from the mountains and about two and a half hours from the coast."

"That's nice." He shook his head. "Is it just me or is it difficult to breathe here?"

"No, it's not just you. We have a lot of smog. And with all the wildfires burning, the air quality is pretty bad."

"I don't think I'd be able to live in it day after day."

"I've thought about moving to the coast many times."

"What stops you?"

She shrugged. "The homes are expensive. Cost of living is higher. My family's here." Of course, now that she'd learned about her biological father, she also had family in Pennsylvania.

"Those are pretty good reasons. But I hate to think staying will be at the cost of your health."

"I know. Not that great of a choice, is it? But it is what it is."

~

Taylor braked for traffic, which was now at a standstill. He glanced over at Candace, who appeared to be having a good time. But he couldn't shake the feeling that he'd made a mistake in coming. Was God sending him a warning?

"Did you enjoy breakfast?"

She smiled. "Yeah, it was great."

"Is LA always this bad?" He gestured toward the freeway congestion all around them.

"It's worse at certain times of day than others. Early Sunday morning is usually a pretty nice time to travel."

"Hmm..." *Everyone stays home from church?* He wouldn't voice his thoughts on why it was probably a good time for traveling.

"Thank you for doing this, Taylor. It really means a lot to me."

"To tell the truth, I've missed you." He glanced her way.

"I've felt the same way."

"May I ask you a pointed question? It might seem somewhat personal." He warned.

"Sure." She laughed a bit nervously. "I can always plead the Fifth, right?"

"I hope you'll answer honestly."

"What's your question?"

"You say your husband attended church faithfully, and your children do as well—"

Her brow shot up. "Why don't I too?"

"Kind of. But my question is a little deeper than that." He met her eyes. "What has kept you back from trusting in Christ?"

"I don't know." She blew out a breath and stared out the window for several quiet seconds. "I guess I just have too many unanswered questions."

"Like what?"

"Well, why do people have to go to church all the time?"

"People who are in love with Jesus *want to* go to church. Church is where you can learn and grow. It's where you meet with other believers who have the same convictions you do—for the most part, anyway."

"So, nobody makes you go?"

He chuckled. "No. I'm not Amish. I attend completely of my own accord. Three times a week, sometimes more."

"I don't get it. Why?"

"Let me explain it this way. When you met Jim, I'm guessing you wanted to learn as much about him as you could. Am I right?"

Candace nodded.

"And when you discovered that you loved him, I'm guessing you wanted to be around him as much as possible. Am I correct?" He continued at her nod. "Well, it's the same way with Jesus. But Jesus is so much more than a mere man. Just trying to fathom His creation and how He loved us enough to willingly die for us, is mind-boggling. You can never learn enough or know enough about Him. It's almost like there is an unquenchable thirst inside you."

"And you find your answers at church?"

"Well, through God's Word, the Bible."

"See, I don't understand that. Can't you just read your Bible at home?"

"I can and I do. But I often get a different perspective from the preacher. Many times, I don't see things that were right in front of me. Things tend to make more sense." He looked over at Candace. Was everything he was saying going straight over her head?

"Yeah, I don't..." She shrugged.

He tamped down his mounting frustration. *God, please open her eyes.* "What were your other questions?"

"If God is so big and powerful, why does He allow suffering?"

"Pain, suffering, all that, is a result of sin. In the Garden of Eden, mankind—Adam and Eve—made their choice when they disobeyed God and ate from the Tree of the Knowledge of Good and Evil. They already knew good. God was good. God *is* good. But they didn't know evil. Instead of trusting God to know what was best, they trusted their own thoughts and feelings. When they ate of that fruit, they brought sin and death into the world. They brought a curse upon themselves and upon their descendants."

"But God can stop it, right?"

"Yes, and He will...eventually. But the events in this world don't happen around our timetable, they happen around God's. He sees all of history *and* the future in just one glance— it's hidden from us. We only know what we see now and what He's said in His Word. We have to trust Him to know what He's doing."

"But what if we *don't* trust Him?"

"That is a choice that each individual has to make. And, like Adam and Eve, we'll have to deal with the consequences of that choice." He frowned.

"I can't understand why He won't just stop it, just stop it all."

Taylor sensed a war waging within her soul. He prayed that truth would win out. "God says in His Word that He is longsuffering toward us, and that it's not His will that any should perish. I think that since God *knows* how terrible Hell actually is, He is giving mankind as many chances as possible.

No matter how bad this earth gets, Hell is going to be much much worse.

"Through Jesus, He has made a way for us to escape the wrath to come—to escape Hell and the Lake of Fire—but some still choose to walk around ignoring God's repeated warnings. One day, when God has most likely had enough, He will return and destroy all evil. But God loves His creation and He does not want anyone to suffer for all eternity."

"But, if He's God, can't He abolish Hell? Can't He just abolish evil?"

"I don't claim to have all the answers, but this is how I see it. God works in the realm of eternity. Human beings have a soul that is eternal, meaning we will last forever. God dwells in perfectness, in righteousness. Heaven is a place of peace and perfection, which means that He cannot allow sin to enter through its gates. If He did allow it, Heaven would become tainted like Earth is now. He won't abolish Hell because He is a God of justice. Hell and the Lake of Fire is the just reward for rejecting Him.

"And that is why God gives us chance after chance to choose Him. Do you understand?"

She shook her head. "I don't know if I agree with Him."

"There's really nothing to agree with, Candace. It is what it is whether we agree or disagree. Truth isn't dependent on us. Adam could have chosen not to believe that he would die, but he did anyway. We don't determine whether truth is truth. It just is."

"I don't think I want to talk about this anymore. Sorry."

He lifted his hands then blew out a breath. "Fine."

"I'm sorry."

"No, it's okay. You're probably on information overload. I have a habit of doing that once in a while."

"So, you're not offended?"

"No. Your relationship with God is between you and God." He *was* disappointed though.

"Oh good." She expelled a breath that he translated as relief. But *he* felt no relief.

She turned to him. "So, have *you* ever been to Medieval Times?"

"Can't say I have."

She squealed. "You're in for a treat!"

Taylor pondered their previous conversation. He realized that he needed to have patience, back off, and give her time. And pray that God would work in her heart as only He could do.

EIGHTEEN

"So, did you enjoy yourself?" Candace grinned as they walked out of the 'castle.'

"I've got to admit, watching sword fighting and eating without utensils was pretty cool. It's too bad our knight didn't win though."

She shrugged. "Maybe next time."

"Next time, huh?" His brow shot up. "Seeing their display of swords and knives was pretty cool too. Maybe someday I'll own a suit of armor."

Her eyes lit up. "That'd be neat."

"Now...to the coast?"

"We've got about an hour before sunset. Sounds good to me."

"Watching the sun plunge into the ocean will be fascinating." He smiled. "Any idea how to get there?"

"Nope. But I'm guessing if we head west we'll eventually run into it."

"That sounds like an adventure we might *not* want to take." He chuckled. "I've heard stories about Los Angeles."

"Well, according to the GPS, it doesn't look like we're too far from Long Beach."

"You ever been there?"

"The town, yes. The actual beach, no. But that's where *The Queen Mary* is located."

"I don't think I'm familiar with that."

"It's an old fancy ship. I think it was British owned. I don't really know too much about it. Just that it's really impressive, probably comparable to the *Titanic*."

"Hmm...sounds interesting." He raised a brow. "So, Long Beach, then?"

"Sure."

NINETEEN

Candace stood next to Taylor's rental car. She'd hate to see him return home, but their time together was up. "Well, that was a really fun birthday surprise. I don't know how to thank you, Taylor."

He grinned. "You just did."

Before meeting Taylor, Candace hadn't even considered dating again and possibly...*remarriage*? But now, being in his company reminded her once again how much she missed that companionship. She hadn't even been sure that guys like Taylor existed—caring, respectful, chivalrous—let alone that they would be interested in her.

The only thing between them was his faith. But that wasn't really an obstacle, was it? After all, she and Jim had lived in harmony for many years with different religious views. She could tolerate attending church every now and then if it meant keeping a husband satisfied. Yep, she was finally ready for something deeper.

He opened the car door. "Well, I guess I should probably get going. Don't want to miss my flight."

"Okay." She stepped close to embrace him and their lips met. Whether on purpose or by accident she wasn't completely sure.

He quickly turned away and released her. "Candace." He grimaced. "I'm sorry. I shouldn't have allowed that."

By accident. Yeah, that's what it was.

He stepped back, putting even more distance between them. "Listen, I had a great time. And I do consider you a good friend. But anything more just isn't going to work between us. I'm sorry. Truly."

A friend? "But wait. I thought..." She frowned. "What's going on, Taylor? We have something here. I know we do. I know *you* know we do. I may have initiated that kiss, but *you* kissed me back."

"I know." He covered his eyes with his hand. "I shouldn't have. It was wrong. It gives false hope and I sincerely apologize."

"Why?"

"I cannot go into a relationship with an unbeliever, that's all there is to it. It would be going against my faith and disobeying God."

"What? But Jim and I—"

"I'm not Jim. I'm sorry. Really. I should go now." He rushed past her, stepped into his SUV, and closed the door. He lifted his hand in a goodbye gesture, but she couldn't bring hers to do the same. She didn't think she'd ever forget the look of regret on his face as he'd closed the door.

She was *so* sure that they'd clicked. They'd connected, hadn't they? She was even pretty certain that she saw a flicker of passion in his eyes. But she was imagining it. She must've been wrong. Dreadfully wrong.

Tears pricked her eyes as she watched Taylor's taillights disappear around the corner, as he drove away from her home and out of her life. For good.

She'd lost him. She'd lost a wonderful man who'd probably never give her the time of day again. And it stunk. It stunk bad.

~

Jackie's excited voice sang over the phone, "So? How'd it go, Mom?"

Candace released an inward groan. "What are you talking about?"

"You know *exactly* what I'm referring to, Miss Trying to Act Clueless!"

"Don't even ask." She groused. "Remind me to never date a man again." She massaged her temples, attempting to dispel her pounding headache.

"*What*? Taylor adores you! I could tell by the way he spoke in his messages." Jackie sighed. "Oh no, what did you do, Mom?"

"What do you mean, what did *I* do? I didn't do anything."

"Well then why did you scare him off? It's Dad, right? You're still in love with Dad."

123

"Jackie...You know I'll always love your dad, but this has nothing to do with him."

"So...what happened?"

"I don't know, really. We had a wonderful day together. He even kissed me. Well, he kissed me *back*."

"Wait. You've kissed him! This is more serious than I thought. *Mom*!"

"It's not serious. It's non-existent."

"Why?"

"Apparently, I'm not religious enough for him."

"What religion is he?"

"Christian, I guess."

"So, he dumped you because you weren't Christian enough?"

"I don't know, Jackie. He just said that it's not going to work."

"So, he came all the way out here to take you to dinner then break up with you."

"We were never a couple, Jackie. We were just friends."

"*Just friends* don't fly across the country to go on a date. *Just friends* don't kiss."

"He said it was a mistake. Besides, I think it was just wishful thinking on my part."

"I'm going to message him and give him a piece of my mind."

"Don't! Don't you dare, Jackie! I'm an adult. I can handle this on my own."

"I don't like the way *he's* handling this. He shouldn't be toying with your emotions like that."

"He wasn't. Now just drop it. *Please*."

"Fine."

"I mean it."

"But Mom, I want you to be happy. And Taylor was so promising. He seemed like such a nice guy."

"He is a nice guy. But he's not *my* guy. Now, can we please just drop it?"

"Okay, Mom."

TWENTY

"Joe." The homeless man, Ralph—who'd first come to the shelter last year—called him over to the table, where he sat next to a woman and three children. "I'd like you to meet my wife, Cathy. And these are our children."

"Hello. It's very nice to meet you." Joe smiled and shook the woman's hand. "I'm Joseph. What are your names?" He asked the children.

"I'm Mitchell," the oldest boy said.

"Sierra." The girl nodded.

"Jaden." The youngest boy seemed more timid than the other two.

"You enjoying that chicken dinner?" Joe grinned.

"Yes, it's very good. Thank you," Cathy said. "And I don't know how to thank you for what you've done for Ralph. It seems like he's a new man now."

Ralph reached over and grasped his wife's hand.

"It isn't what I have done, but what Christ has done. Only God can change a man's heart," Joe deflected.

"But you connected us again through the Christmas tree program back in December." She nodded. "I'm grateful."

"That program was actually my wife's idea." Joe smiled at the thought of sharing the news with Anna.

"Please share our gratitude with her."

"I will." Joe nodded.

"I'll be leaving the shelter today. Cathy said I can come back home now." Ralph smiled.

"That's great to hear." Joe frowned. Would Ralph return to his previous lifestyle without support? He hoped not. "Will you continue to attend the RU meetings?"

"Sure will." Ralph nodded. "I found a church near our hometown that offers the classes. We plan to attend church there as well."

"I'm so happy to hear that, Ralph. God sure is good, isn't He?"

"He's beyond good, Joe."

"Remember, we're always here for you. Keep our number close by and call sometime to let me know how you're doing. Keep God first and you can't go wrong."

"Will do, Joe." Ralph smiled. "Thanks."

As Joe bid the family farewell, his heart soared. *Thank You, Gott, for letting them find their way to You.*

~

Candace smiled as she appeared on the screen of Taylor's tablet. "To what do I owe the pleasure of this surprise chat?"

Taylor stayed out of the camera's view, but he still watched Candace from his end of the table. How he missed her! But he really couldn't see any way around the obstacles in their relationship. If she wasn't interested in God, he couldn't pursue a relationship with her. Period.

He sighed and stood up, giving Anna and Joe the opportunity to share their news.

"Look who the stork dropped off!" Mary squealed excitedly.

"Who?" Candace acted surprised.

"My baby brothers! Sammy and Jakey!" She bounced excitedly. "Momma let me hold 'em."

"Really? How exciting!"

Joe and Anna held up the babies behind Mary.

"Oh, they're precious! Congratulations, guys."

"*Denki.*" Anna sounded tired.

One of the babies began crying.

"I think he's getting hungry. Again." Joe said, admiring his little one.

"Well, I better let you go then. Joe, make sure Anna doesn't overdo it. She looks like she could use some rest." That was Candace. Thoughtful. Caring.

"Goodbye."

The video clicked off.

"Thanks for letting us use your device, Taylor. Those things are pretty handy."

"Yeah, they are. I wish Harv could've been here too." Taylor frowned.

"Maybe next time."

"Yeah."

~

"You know what I'm thankful for? I'm thankful for you. I think I should marry you someday." Harv mused aloud, taking a bite of the pumpkin pie *Mammi* had just served him. She made the best pies he'd ever tasted. And at Thanksgiving, she made enough for them to taste a different kind for a week.

Mammi gently reached her hand across the table and placed it over his. She stared into his eyes for several silent seconds and lifted a small smile. Sometimes it felt like this woman could see into his soul. "You and I both know that can never be." She squeezed his hand then let go.

"You're right. I wish you weren't, blast it, but you're right." He shook his head. "Don't seem right, though. Does it?"

Mammi shrugged.

"Seems like a man ought to marry anyone he chooses. If a man and woman care about each other, love each other…" He shook his head. "It's no use, is it?"

"I'm afraid not, Harv." He read her pained expression. "It's just the way things have to be."

"I don't like the way things have to be. Hardly seems fair."

"You and I both know that fairness has nothing to do with it. You have chosen to live one way, I have chosen another. It's as simple—and as complicated—as that."

"But you believe in God, and I believe in God. That should be enough. Shouldn't it?"

"Our *g'may* is pretty fast, but I don't see any Amish group allowing one of their own to marry an *Englischer*. It's just not gonna happen." *Mammi* shook her head. "Either both need to be *Englisch*, or both Amish."

Harv frowned.

"I know you do not wish to become Plain. And I cannot bear to be shunned from my own *grossdochder* and her family. But we can remain friends, *ain't so*?"

Harv stood and took his plate to the sink, immersing it in water. He didn't want *Mammi* to see his unshed tears. He despised their presence.

Mammi placed her hand on his shoulder blade. She knew. She knew their situation was hopeless and there was nothing either of them could do about it.

He turned and pulled her into his arms, but he wouldn't dare look into her eyes. He briefly kissed the side of her prayer *kapp*, then released her and, with slumped shoulders walked out of the kitchen, leaving a chunk of his heart standing by the sink.

TWENTY-ONE

Early December, Present Day

"Wow! I can't believe the weather is turning again. It seems the years just fly by too fast." Harv rubbed his hands together.

"Can you believe it's been almost a year since you learned that you had a *dochder*?" Joe mused.

"It's crazy. I wish I could see her more." Harv sighed. "But her life is in California."

Joe's brow shot up. "You sure about that?"

"What do you mean?"

"I don't know. I thought maybe she and Taylor had something going on."

"I mind my own business." Harv shrugged.

Joe chuckled. "Since when?"

"I *have* talked to Taylor," Harv admitted. "They have a friendship of sorts."

"Well, that's something."

"He wants more, but she isn't a believer. And I think she's scared."

"Of what?"

"Probably of losing another loved one."

"But death is a natural part of life. We can't shut out all the good things in life—the blessings—because of the bad, or because we're afraid of being hurt. I couldn't imagine not having Anna in my life. If I would have given up after I lost my *aldi,* Mary, I would have missed out on so many blessings. Love. Joy. *Kinner.*" He smiled.

Harv smirked. "You're welcome."

"So...why don't you encourage your *dochder* the way you did me?"

"You don't think she'll suspect an ulterior motive?"

"Is there something wrong with a *vatter* wanting to be near his *dochder?* Besides that, if anything ever does happen between her and Taylor, he could move to California. Hasn't he already been out there to see her?"

Harv sighed. "You're right."

"But *first* I think we need to pray that *Der Herr* gets a hold of your *dochder's* heart."

Harv agreed.

~

Joe's head shot up when Mary's scream ricocheted through the air. He immediately dropped the lead line to his mare and bolted toward the house.

He stumbled inside. His wife was nowhere in sight. "Anna? Where are you?"

"I'm in here. In the bathroom." The distress in her voice caused his heart to lurch.

He poked his head through the bathroom door. His little girl soaked in the tub. "What's going on, *Schatzi*?"

"Mary's sick. She feels hot."

He kneeled next to the bathtub, reached into the cool water surrounding Mary, dipped a washcloth into it, and then placed it on Mary's forehead. "Does that feel better, *liebling*?"

Mary attempted to smile and speak, but all that passed her lips was a groan.

Joe's worried expression met his wife's. "We need to get her to the ER. They can give her an IV. I'll go call Taylor for a ride."

"I'll just have Mary stay in the bath until Taylor arrives."

"*Jah*, that'll be *gut*." Joe rushed out the door.

~

Joe glanced down at Mary. She looked so frail and helpless lying in the large hospital bed with an IV strapped to her arm. At least she was sleeping now.

"What do you think is wrong with her, doctor?" Joseph watched intently as the doctor checked his daughter's vital signs.

"Could be the flu." He moved his stethoscope to Mary's chest. "I hear some congestion. It's most likely just an upper respiratory infection. You need not worry, Mr. Bender, your daughter should be fine soon enough."

"Mary has had very few sicknesses," Anna interjected, stroking Mary's hand. She glanced at the twins, contently sleeping in their covered stroller across the room. They'd attempted to shield them from Mary and needed to take them to the waiting room as soon as the doctor finished examining Mary. They couldn't afford for the other *kinner* to contract something too.

"Then count your blessings." The doctor shrugged. "Your daughter is certainly not the first to get sick. I wouldn't worry."

Joe watched the doctor leave the room, then looked to his wife. He read the distress in her face, saw the unshed tears of worry in her eyes. He pulled her close and kissed the top of her head.

"You take the *bopplin* out, I will stay with Mary." He caressed her face. "I will come down to the waiting room in a while."

She nodded.

"Will you call and see if Rachel or *Mammi* can come? We can take turns staying with Mary, but I'd like to be with *mei fraa* for a while too. And it's probably not good to keep the *bopplin* here in the hospital, *no*?"

"We don't want them to get sick, but I'd like to be with Mary too. I don't want her to get scared," she whispered.

"She will most likely sleep." He looked to Mary again, whose cheeks were flushed bright pink. She seemed so small. So frail. So vulnerable.

Never in his life had he felt so helpless. He was supposed to be the leader of this family. The provider. The protector. Yet, in this moment, he felt like an utter failure.

Please, Gott, help Mary. Help us.

TWENTY-TWO

"Mr. and Mrs. Bender, I'd like a word with you." The doctor held a clipboard in his hand, a concerned look clouding his expression.

"What is it, doctor?" Joseph frowned.

"It's about Mary. Her respiratory condition seems to have worsened and it's spreading to her lungs. I'm afraid she's contracting pneumonia."

"That is bad, *jah*?" Anna twisted her hands together. Joe rubbed her back, attempting to comfort her.

"It is, but we *are* treating it. I do feel like I need to warn you, though. Pneumonia can and does claim the lives of thousands of children each year. Of course, that is the worst-case scenario. The best case is that she's over it quickly and she can return home."

"You're saying our Mary can die?" Anna sucked in a sob.

"It's a possibility, but not a probability."

"You're saying it probably *won't* happen." Joseph affirmed, hoping Anna would be relieved by the fact.

"That's right." The doctor nodded. "She's getting the best treatment possible."

~

Anna couldn't sleep. Not with Mary at the hospital and her and Joe many miles away. "I feel like I should be there with her, Joe. What if she...?"

Anna shook her head, unwilling to voice their reality. Yet, she needed to come to terms with the facts, whether she wanted to or not. "I wouldn't be able to bear it if she died alone."

"She's not going to die, *Schatzi*. They would call us if she got worse. And she won't be alone. Harv and *Mammi* are there right now. *Der Herr* is with her too." He rubbed her arm. "You have the little ones. They're too young to be without their *mamm, ain't so*? You need to feed them."

"I know. I just wish I could be in two places at once. Mary needs me too."

"Would you like it better if we rented a hotel room closer to the hospital? It would be pretty expensive but you'd be able to see Mary in between the *bopplin's* feedings."

"Could we do that?"

"If it will make you happy, we can, *jah*. I have some money saved up." He grimaced. "I was saving it for emergencies. I guess this qualifies."

~

Harv entered the waiting room, excited to tell Joe the news. Anna sat on one of the chairs with the twins in their stroller nearby. It was a shame they didn't live closer to the hospital. But Harv had a solution for that.

"Miss Anna! How are those babies?" He sauntered near and offered a hug.

"They're *gut*."

"Is Joe with Mary?"

"*Jah*. She's in room three twenty now. Just go down the hall and turn right."

"Okie dokie. Be right back, pretty lady." He winked.

Harv pushed the door open to Mary's hospital room.

Joe turned at his entrance. "Harv! I'm so glad to see you."

He moved toward little Mary's bed. "She gettin' any better?"

Joe nodded. "Still has a fever and some congestion. But her fever's gone down some."

Harv grinned.

"What? What are you beaming about?" Joe shook his head. He always could tell when Harv was up to something.

"I have a solution for some of your troubles. Or Taylor does, I should say."

"Which is?"

"Taylor offered to bring his trailer out here for you and Miss Anna to use. You could keep it in the parking lot and be closer to Mary. Anna can stay out there with the babies and Rachel and *Mammi* can take turns babysitting. We can bring Little Joe and Mandy by too and they could stay a night so they don't think their folks have forgotten them."

"Oh, Harv, that would be *wunderbaar*."

"Save you from havin' to spend your money at a hotel too."

"*Der Herr* is *gut*! Anna will be so excited."

~

They'd turned in for the night, and Anna was thankful for the use of Taylor's travel trailer, but she knew it would be impossible for her to sleep. How could she when their precious daughter was in that hospital fighting for her life?

In spite of feeling loved and protected in Joe's arms, the comfort she sought failed to materialize. *I can't do this, Lord. This trial is too much. Please. Please don't take Mary from us. I beg You!*

Anna's body trembled, although she tried to conceal her fears from her husband.

"Shh...it's okay, *Schatzi*." Joe attempted to console her, gently running his hands through her hair.

"I think we should be there with her right now." She brushed a tear away.

"She's asleep now, *lieb*. She'll most likely be asleep for hours. You need your rest too. You have to stay healthy for Mary and the *bobblin*."

"What if she doesn't make it, Joseph? What if we lose her?" Tears streamed down her face as she sobbed. "I don't think I'd be able to handle it. I can't lose our baby, Joe. I can't."

"It's not up to us, *Schatzi*. We have to trust *Der Herr*. Let's hope for the best, *jah*?"

How could he have so much confidence?

"Do you think it was a mistake naming her Mary?"

Joe sat up now and flipped the switch on the lamp beside the bed. He pulled her close and studied her face. "What do you mean, babe?"

"I mean, your Mary, the one you were engaged to. She died young, *jah*?"

"*Jah*...and?"

Anna shook her head, not really wanting to voice her concerns. But if she couldn't share her deepest thoughts with her husband, who could she share them with?

"What? You don't think we cursed our *dochder* by giving her the name Mary, do you?"

She shrugged. "I don't know. Doesn't it seem a little coincidental?"

"*Nee*, Anna. Not to me. Mary's death has nothing to do with this." He sighed. "I know our people can be superstitious, but I can assure you that the two incidences are not related in the least. Just look at all the Marys in the Bible. Mary is a *sehr gut* name. It is the name of our Saviour's mother."

Anna nodded. "*Jah*, you are right."

Joseph sighed. "I fear you are not getting enough rest."

"It's hard for me to sleep."

"Then I will pray for *Der Herr* to take away your fears and give you peace." He stroked her cheek.

"*Denki*."

He lightly kissed her lips. "*Gott* will see us through this, *Lieb*. I have faith that He will heal our *dochder*. And if He doesn't, we will still trust Him. We will still follow Him. We will still serve Him. He *always* knows best. Always. We don't know whether *any* of us will be here tomorrow. But we're here today. Let's thank God for today and trust Him for tomorrow."

She gazed into her husband's eyes. "*Ich liebe dich*, Joseph."

"I love you too, *Schatzi*." He leaned close and kissed her, lingering until she'd nearly forgotten their present troubles.

TWENTY-THREE

"*D*at, will you bring the blanket I made for Baby Jesus?" Mary adjusted her position in her hospital bed.

Joe frowned. "The one you made for Christmas last year?"

"*Jah*. Is it at the shelter?"

"I would imagine it's with the Christmas decorations. What do you need it for, *lieb*?" He lightly stroked her fine hair.

"I want to sleep with it. 'Cuz if I fall asleep and wake up in Heaven, I want to give Baby Jesus the blanket I made for Him."

"I don't think you're going to Heaven just yet, but I will bring the blanket." Joseph and Anna shared a saddened look. Neither one of them corrected Mary or informed her that Jesus would no longer be a baby in Heaven. Somehow, they knew that God would welcome this sweet girl with her heart of gold, and the gift that came from it, with open arms when the time came.

Anna prayed once again, thanking God for blessing their home with Mary, and the joy she brought with her everywhere she went. She was doing her best to take Joe's advice—to have faith for today and not worry about tomorrow.

~

"I have an idea." Anna smiled at Mary. "Since *Dat* is at the shelter getting your blanket, and *Mammi* and Harv are watching the *bopplin*, why don't I read you one of the books I brought?"

"You brought books?" Mary's large eyes sparkled.

"Yep." She patted the canvas bag over her shoulder and dug into it, bringing out several titles. "Which one would you like me to read?"

Mary studied the books intently, as though trying to guess what was inside by their covers. "How about this one?"

"*A Christmas Carol*? That's a really good one."

Anna settled in next to Mary on the hospital bed, holding her close and cherishing each moment. She began reading.

"Why do you think Mr. Scrooge is so grumpy?"

Anna set the book down and looked at Mary. "Well, it's probably because he's all alone."

"I think it's because he never gives presents to anybody. I know that when I give things away, it makes me happy inside. I couldn't think of not being happy inside. But, if I wasn't happy, I would just go to the soup kitchen and help out Uncle Harvey. It's always lots of fun helpin' in the soup kitchen."

"Harvey *is* fun to be around, isn't he? I liked him from the moment I met him and your daddy."

"Where did you meet 'em?"

"Your daddy and Uncle Harvey were living on the streets like a lot of the homeless people at the shelter."

Deep concern marked Mary's features. "Were they sad like some of the people that come into the soup kitchen?"

"*Jah.*"

Mary brightened. "But you made them happy, ain't so?"

"I think Jesus made them happy."

"How?"

"Well, one day, I was in town and I accidentally bumped into your daddy. He looked very sad and cold, and he didn't have *gut* clothes on."

Mary shook her head. "How come?"

"Because he didn't have a family around."

"You mean he didn't have no *fraa* or *mamm* to make him clothes?"

"Nope. His *mamm* lived far away. And your daddy was in the *bann.*"

Mary's eyes grew wide. "*Dat* was in the *bann*?"

Perhaps she shouldn't have shared that information with her daughter just yet. The last thing she needed was a barrage of questions that Mary was too young to hear the answers to.

She quickly changed the subject. "So, *Der Herr* prompted me to take your daddy and Uncle Harvey some food."

"What does *prompted* mean?"

"It means that God placed something in my heart."

"Like He told you to give Daddy food?"

"Pretty much."

"Sometimes God *prompted* me to give people food at the shelter."

"God prompts you too?" Anna smiled. "And you do, right?"

Mary nodded, then her brow lowered. "How come they didn't go to the soup kitchen?"

"The soup kitchens are only in the bigger cities. It was too far to walk, especially in the snow. And they didn't have a buggy." She gently stroked Mary's soft hair. "Anyway, I started bringing the food every day and we became *gut* friends."

Mary smiled. "And then you and Daddy fell in love and got hitched?"

"Eventually, yes."

"I'm so glad you did. Otherwhile, you wouldn't have me!"

Anna chuckled. "I think you mean *otherwise.* And you're right. Mommy and Daddy are very happy to have you and your brothers and sister."

"Can we finish the book now?"

"May we. And yes, we will. But first, I think you might want to know about a surprise."

Mary gasped. "A surprise?"

"Do you remember Candace?"

"Uncle Harvey's *dochder*?"

Anna nodded. "She's coming to visit and she's staying till Christmas."

"I like Miss Candace."

"I do too." Anna smiled.

"I think Taylor likes her too." Mary grinned.

Anna shook her head. Sometimes Mary was too perceptive for her own good.

TWENTY-FOUR

Harvard glanced at Candace as they walked down the sidewalk. "It was good of you to come out early to help out Joe and Anna with their little ones. I'm glad you'll be here for Christmas."

Candace smiled. "It's my pleasure. But it *is* nice to get a break like this once in a while. I enjoy window shopping."

Harvard frowned as he pointed to a Santa Claus display. "I never did understand why people lie to their kids. I was mad at my folks for quite a while when I discovered Santa weren't real."

"Yeah, Jim was against it too. He'd said that if we lie to our kids about Santa being real and later tell them the truth, then they might just think Jesus isn't real either."

"Sounds like your husband was a smart man."

She swallowed. "He was."

"It seems to me like folks set their hearts on the wrong things nowadays."

"For example?" Candace smiled, enjoying this time as she walked through downtown with her father.

"Well, could be anything, I reckon. But take Christmas, for instance. How many folks celebrate Christmas without Christ?"

"A lot, probably. But not everybody believes in Jesus."

"See, that makes no sense to me. We have a holiday that centers around the birth of the Saviour of the world, yet people don't believe in Him." He shook his head. "That's like China having a big 'ol fancy celebration for the Fourth of Ju-ly or eatin' a mess of grub on Thanksgiving. It makes no sense."

"You have a point, I guess. But doesn't it seem like some who call themselves Christians aren't even celebrating for the right reasons?"

"Yep, I see what you're gettin' at. People can go too far with things. Anytime *anything* is put above the Good Lord, it becomes an idol. The sin ain't in celebratin' a holiday, it's in *worshippin'* a holiday. Or anything, for that matter. It's an issue of the heart. If your heart ain't right, then what's the point?"

Candace thought for a moment. Was *her* heart in the right place? Why *did* she celebrate Christmas?

"I guess you're right, Harvard."

He huffed. "Can we quit all that *Harvard* nonsense? You're makin' me feel old."

Candace laughed. "What would you like me to call you then?"

152

"Oh, I don't know. Reckon I never did have no one to call me Dad. Joe's the closest thing I ever had to a son."

Candace smiled, then reached for his hand. "Then Dad it is."

Candace's cell phone rang and she pulled it from her purse. "Hello?"

Harv frowned, waiting for her to end the call.

"Oh, no." She covered her mouth. "Okay, we'll come right away."

She clicked off the phone.

"What is it?" Her father frowned.

"It's Mary. She's taken a turn for the worse."

A SECRET CHRISTMAS

TWENTY-FIVE

"*Ach*, Jacob, Rachel, you're here. *Denki* for coming." Joe nodded to Anna's cousins and ushered them toward Mary's hospital bed.

"How's she doing?" Rachel came near to where Mary lay.

"At first, she seemed to be getting better. But now, it seems like she's getting weaker every hour." Anna couldn't help the tears that moistened the corners of her eyes, something she'd been doing a lot more of lately. She desperately wanted to trust God, to trust His will for their lives. But watching your baby girl die made one question God's ways. Why would He let poor Mary go through this? Why didn't He heal her when Anna had prayed thus time and time again?

"You know, a thought came to me this morning." Rachel's comforting hand on her shoulder helped ease some of her tension. "In Paradise, we used to go to Danika Yoder when we were sick. She learned all about herbs and natural medicine from her uncle, Philip King."

Anna shook her head. "*Mammi* has given her herbs, but they don't seem to be working."

"Maybe Danika knows of something that *will* work. It couldn't hurt to try, could it?"

"We may not have time." Anna brushed a tear away.

"If you want, I can have Jacob call her right now. It's only an hour by car. She could be here before evening."

"*Jah*, okay. I'll need to talk to Joseph first, though."

"It's fine with me, *Schatzi*," Joe chimed in.

Rachel nodded with confidence. "If anyone knows what to do, Danika will. She's dealt with all kinds of sickness."

"I hope you're right."

~

"Since they've had Mary adequately hydrated, do you know if an enema has been done?" Danika asked Joe and Anna.

"An enema? I don't think so," Joe answered. "Why would they do that?"

"An enema is one of the quickest ways to remove toxins from the body and bring down a fever."

"I didn't know that." Anna said.

"You might want to see if they'll give her one. They used to do it all the time as routine in hospitals, but not anymore."

Joe nodded. "Okay, we'll suggest that to the nurse."

Danika placed her hand on Mary's forehead. "Has she been taking any Echinacea or Elderberry?"

"No, I don't think so." Joe looked to Anna for confirmation.

"Okay, I checked the medications they have her on and there are no contraindications with these herbs. Would you like me to give her some? I have a children's variety that will go down easy." Danika looked to Joe and Anna.

"*Jah*. Whatever will help her to get better." Anna nodded.

"These herbs will boost her immune system and help fight off whatever she has." She took a dropper bottle out of her bag and squeezed the contents of the dropper into the side of Mary's mouth, a little at a time.

Mary's eyes flitted open for just a second, then closed again.

Danika handed the bottle to Anna. "She needs this much," she showed her the proper amount on the glass dropper, "at least five times each day."

"We will make sure she gets it. *Denki*, Danika."

~

When Taylor entered Mary's hospital room, Candace thought her heart might stop beating. She hadn't seen him in person since he'd visited California in July. Man, he was just as handsome as ever. She averted her gaze and noticed he did the same.

"Candace." He nodded.

Well, at least he'd acknowledged her presence.

She nodded back.

"You just missed the herb doctor," Joe informed Taylor.

"How's she doing?" Taylor asked.

Joe frowned. "Not that great. But Danika is confident the herbs will help her."

"I have an idea. May we pray for her?"

"Sure. But we've been praying for her constantly."

"I meant as a group. What if we had everyone come into her room and we all pray together?" Taylor suggested.

Joe looked to Anna, then to Candace.

"Sure, why not?" Joe shrugged.

Taylor smiled. "Okay, I'll get everyone who is in the waiting room and let the nurses know what's going on so they don't freak out. We may be forced to do it in the waiting room. Or maybe we can sneak everyone in one at a time."

Candace was almost positive he'd just winked at her. She watched as he disappeared.

A few moments later, Anna, Joe, Taylor, Harv, *Mammi*, Candace, and Danika all assembled around Mary's bed.

"Let's hold hands," Taylor suggested.

They did, and he began praying aloud. "Dear God in Heaven, we know that Your ears are open to our prayers. Thank You for Your goodness and Your mercy and for hearing our petitions. We come before You right now, in Jesus' name, and ask that You touch little Mary's body and heal her. I ask that You make her well so she can spend Christmas at home with her family. Lord, this little girl has a big heart. And I have no doubt that she will grow up to serve You, if You'll grant her the opportunity. Thank You, Lord. Amen."

"Amen." Everyone said in unison, most wiping away tears.

Candace looked straight into Taylor's eyes, her own still misted over. "Thank you."

TWENTY-SIX

Taylor's interest had been piqued. He'd never known much about herbs or natural medicine. He'd always assumed it was just one of those fads that came and went. But the fact that his Amish friends believed so much in them had him curious.

He entered the waiting room and sought out Danika. "Danika, do you mind me asking some questions?"

"No, about what?" She smiled.

He took a seat beside her. "Well, how did you learn about herbs?"

"My *dat*, Uncle Philip, he taught me everything I know. I used to want to be a medical doctor."

Taylor frowned. "What made you change your mind? Or was it something the Amish didn't allow?"

"Well, I grew up *Englisch* in California."

Taylor's brow rose. He thought of Candace. "I never would have guessed. You look so Amish. But now that I think about it, I can tell there's something different about you."

"Yeah. My mother left the Amish as a young woman in *rumspringa* and married my father. He was Hispanic, which is probably why I seem a little different. My mother died when I was eight. And then my Dad got cancer. He wasn't very sick or anything, so you wouldn't even have known. But the doctor said that if he didn't get the treatment they offered—chemo— that he'd be dead in six months. So he started on the chemo.

"I noticed something very peculiar. As soon as he began the treatments, that the doctor said would *help* him, he got worse. But the doctor assured us that he would eventually get better. He never did. Dad's health only went downhill until we put him to rest in the grave." She brushed away a tear. "I was thirteen—and devastated. That's when I went to live with my aunt and uncle, who adopted me."

"Wow, I'm so sorry. You went through a lot at such a young age." He shook his head. "That sounds so much like what happened to my wife. She died two years ago. So, are you insinuating it was the chemo that likely killed your father?"

"I didn't know it then, but I'm almost positive now. After that, I had a talk with Uncle Philip. He knew all about the devastation that chemotherapy causes in the body. He explained to me how chemo *does* kill cancer, but it also kills the healthy cells too. If your healthy cells are destroyed, your body has no way to fight disease.

"Anyway, he'd done a lot of research. He said that for reliable, honest cancer research, one has to seek out independent sources. Otherwise, you get biased information that is actually funded by the pharmaceutical companies. Or certain 'cancer awareness' or 'cancer research' groups that earn millions of dollars getting donations. And that's the problem, why there will never be a true cure for cancer."

He frowned. "What do you mean?"

"Well, let's just say that the cancer industry is a multi-billion-dollar industry. There already are several non-drug treatments that work for cancer. But imagine if everyone were to seek out natural cures—things they could easily grow themselves very inexpensively in their own backyard—the cancer industry would go bankrupt overnight and lose all their money. Think of how many jobs would be lost."

Taylor sighed, not wanting to consider the possibility. "So, you think they'd rather let people *die* than acknowledge a real cure?"

"I'm sure a lot of people in the industry are sincere and *do* want to help people. And they believe they are helping because every once in a while, someone survives. Most are just ignorant about what truly fights and heals cancer, but it's not their fault. They aren't properly taught about it in schools.

"But if you think about it, profits over people is nothing new. The Bible says 'the love of money is the root of all evil.' If you want to know why some things are the way they are, you need only to 'follow the yellow brick road.'"

"That's so sad." Taylor lifted a brow. "I'm dying for something to drink. Would you care to join me in the cafeteria for some tea or juice?"

"Sure. But I'll just have water." They walked side-by-side down the hallway. "I often wonder if my father would still be alive today if he'd rejected the chemo treatments and sought out an alternative route."

"So, do natural things *really* work?" They entered the cafeteria and Taylor found a vending machine. He placed his money into the slot and selected a bottle of apple juice.

Danika followed him to a small table and they sat down. "Well, each person is different. Some people are already too far gone to do anything. I don't think my dad was, though, because he'd had very few symptoms until he began treatment. It's almost like the chemo made it spread throughout his body faster. I honestly think he would have lived longer if he'd done nothing at all.

"But everyone *does* have to die sometime. To answer your question though, yes, many people *do* find wonderful success with natural remedies. To me, it makes perfect sense that they would. Think about it. God made our bodies from the dust of the earth. Plants come from the earth as well. I believe that if we give our bodies what they need, our bodies will heal themselves.

"Most cancer patients have a weakened immune system. Chemo only weakens it more. I think that if we can build a strong immune system, our bodies can fight off anything that comes their way. It's just a matter of knowing what our bodies need and what to avoid."

"And how would a person find out what they need?"

"Well, if a person is sick, you can almost guarantee that their body is in desperate need of a cleanse. We eat so much junk these days that has little to no nourishment, that our poor bodies don't know how to process it. If we cleanse, it will flush out the toxins that have found weakened areas of the body and pocketed themselves there. That's basically what a tumor is—toxins that have built up and hidden themselves away trying to protect the rest of the body. Our bodies can only take so much abuse.

"If we go back to the Bible, in the beginning, we'll see that God gives us the perfect diet for our bodies, and it's entirely plant-based. If you look at the healthiest cultures in the world, you'll see that their diet is primarily plant-based."

"Wow. That makes a lot of sense."

"It does, doesn't it?" Danika nodded. "I feel fortunate to have learned everything I know. Although there is still so much more I could learn."

"Well, I'm just glad that you do know about health. Everyone seems so sick these days."

"I know. And eating right isn't easy for most people. I can hardly keep my husband Eli away from his chips." Danika laughed. "I'm just glad he doesn't fight me on the carrot juice. I aim to keep him around for as long as possible."

"Carrot juice?" Taylor grimaced.

"It's not as bad as it sounds, trust me. Unless you buy the store-bought stuff. But freshly-made juice from sweet raw carrots is actually delicious."

"It is?"

"Yes, everyone should try it. And if they don't care much for carrots, they can always mask the flavor by adding in other things like apples or whatever."

"Hmm...that sounds interesting. So you just throw the carrots into the blender?"

"No." She smiled. "You must use a juicer. A juicer will leave enough of the fiber to assist in cleansing, but will retain the nutrients. It's kind of like a vitamin shot."

"Do you have a business card? I'd love to discuss this more or have someone to call if I have any health questions." He tossed his empty container into the trash receptacle.

Danika dug into her bag. "Here's my card. We're in Paradise."

"Paradise? You don't happen to know Jonathan Fisher, do you?" "Do I ever!" Danika burst out laughing.

TWENTY-SEVEN

Candace was happy to find Mary alert and looking better each day. But something seemed off with the little girl. She didn't seem like the cheerful girl Candace had come to know last year and throughout their video chats. "Your mother and father say that you're usually a happy little girl."

"*Jah*." Mary sighed, as though she carried the weight of the world on her tiny shoulders.

"Will you tell me why you look so sad then?"

"I heard Momma and *Dat* talking with the doctor the other day. They thought I was sleeping but I was just resting my eyes. The doctor said I might not be here at Christmas." Mary frowned. "If I'm not here, then where will I be?"

Candace coughed. How could she answer this question? It certainly wasn't her place to inform the little girl that she'd been on the verge of death. "I...you should probably talk with your mommy about that, honey."

"He was talking about Heaven, huh?"

Candace's smile pulled tight. "You don't need to worry about any of it. Okay, honey?"

"But I wanted to get Momma and *Dat* something really nice for Christmas since I can't help Momma make anything. And Uncle Harvey and *Mammi* too. If I'm not here, I won't be able to."

An overwhelming sense of compassion for this selfless child exploded in her chest. "Oh, sweetheart. That's very thoughtful to think of your parents, but they will understand if you can't get them anything."

"But I want them to have a super special Christmas. Because if I'm not here, they will be sad." She frowned. "And I don't want Momma and *Dat* to be sad, 'cuz I'll be happy with Jesus. I want them to be happy too."

"You're a really sweet little girl, you know that? But I think that you are going to live for a long, long time. I'll tell you what. You let me know what you want to get them and I'll go and buy it."

"But I don't have any money."

"I will be happy to buy what you'd like to get for them, and then I'll bring it here and you can help me wrap it. How does that sound?"

"You want to wrap up a milk goat?" Mary's eyes bulged.

A milk goat? Candace laughed. "No, I guess not. But we can get her a pretty bow and tie it around her neck."

Mary nodded in satisfaction. "You don't think they'll let you bring it to the hospital?"

Candace smiled and shook her head. "Probably not, sweetheart. I'll tell you what I'll do. How about I take a picture of it with my phone, then you'll be able to see it too?"

"*Jah.* That sounds *gut.*" Mary leaned forward and wrapped her tiny arms around Candace's neck. "*Denki* so much! It'll be the best Christmas ever!"

"Are you *sure* you want to get them a goat for Christmas?"

"Sure and certain. It can be for everyone. *Dat* loves to drink goat milk with his whoopie pies and Momma sometimes buys it for the *bopplin*. And my *bruder* and *schweschder* would like a goat to play with." Her eyes sparkled with excitement. "It's perfect."

Tears pricked Candace's eyes. How different the world was when viewed from the eyes of a little girl.

~

"Taylor, hello. Thank you for meeting me." Candace stepped off the porch of Joe and Anna's house, where she'd been staying the past few days, and approached Taylor as he exited his vehicle.

"It's good to see you, Candace." He smiled, but she could see the hesitance in his eyes, as though he wasn't sure how to act around her.

"I'd like to be friends, if that's possible. Even if nothing more comes of our relationship, I would like to be able to talk to you and spend a little bit of time together. No strings attached." She swallowed, trying to convey her sincerity. "I've missed our companionship."

"I've missed you too, Candace. And yes, I would like to be friends and dispel this awkwardness." He held her gaze for a moment before glancing away and clearing his throat. "So, you said you had a favor to ask?"

She nodded. "I was speaking with Mary a couple days ago and she said she wanted to get her family a special present for Christmas, something they will all use and enjoy."

"Like what?"

"A milk goat."

Taylor's brows lifted. "She wants a *goat*?"

"She does." Candace laughed. "She says everyone will like it because then they can have goat milk and the little ones will have a pet."

"Pretty sound logic."

"Mm...hm. I visited a goat farm just down the road and took pictures of the goats. Yesterday, I showed them to Mary so she could pick out which one she wanted. I wanted it to be her choice, not mine. Will you go with me out to the farm to purchase it?"

"Sure. Yeah. We can do that."

She nodded. "Okay, good. I felt a little awkward going on my own. I would have asked my father, but I wasn't too sure he'd be able to keep the secret."

"You're probably right." He laughed. "Should we go then? Are you ready now?"

"Yep." She smiled.

They both entered Taylor's Explorer and Candace directed him to the farm. They reached it in a matter of minutes.

The second Candace opened the car door she was greeted by dozens of bleating goats begging for her attention. She approached the fence containing the creatures. "Hi, guys. Remember me?"

The owner of the farm approached. "Ms. Dixon, how nice to see you again. So... have you decided which goat you want?"

"Yes, sir. I'd like to purchase little Christmas."

"Wonderful. If you'll come inside with me, I can show you her paperwork."

Candace and Taylor followed the man into his house and quickly filled out the necessary paperwork. She purchased the goat and shook the owner's hand. "I was wondering if it would be possible to keep her here until Christmas Eve? It would be much easier to keep Christmas a secret if she's here."

"That's fine. If you'd like, I can deliver her to you around, say, five o'clock?"

"That sounds wonderful. How much do you charge for delivery?"

The older man grinned. "No charge. You can consider it my Christmas gift to you."

"Thank you so much. That's so kind of you." Candace grinned. "Here. Let me write down the address for you." She quickly jotted down the information and handed it to the man.

Taylor spoke up. "Would you mind if we take a look at Christmas? I'd like to see her."

"Of course. She's in the barn. I'll show you."

Candace and Taylor followed the man to a small stall where a black and white goat stood munching on hay.

"Christmas, huh? Why name her Christmas instead of something like Charcoal or Oreo or Spotty?" Taylor mused.

"Well, you see, Christmas was born just last year on Christmas morning. I had my family and grandchildren all here for the holiday and the little ones were out playing in the snow when they found that little Christmas here was born." The man shrugged. "After that, there really wasn't any choice in the matter."

"When I told Mary her name, she said it had to be this one." Candace smiled, reaching out to pet the goat's neck. "I hope she gets the chance to see her in person."

"Me too." Taylor stroked the goat's forehead. "Me too."

TWENTY-EIGHT

"What is today?" Mary asked Anna and Joe.

"It's the twenty-third. Two days before Christmas." Joe smiled.

"I feel lots better now. Can I go home?"

Anna looked to Joe and reached a hand to Mary's forehead. She then felt her daughter's cheek. "I don't think she has a fever anymore, Joe." Her eyes danced with excitement.

"Really?" Joe smiled.

"I feel *gut*, *Dat*. I'm not tired anymore."

Joe looked to Anna. "I'll call for the doctor."

About twenty minutes later, the doctor finally arrived and examined Mary's condition. He looked to Mary and smiled. "I don't see any reason why you can't spend Christmas at home this year."

"Really?" Mary squealed. "I get to go home?"

"You sure do, sweetheart. But I want you to know that there are a lot of friends that are going to miss you here." He grinned. "But that doesn't mean that we want you to come back." The doctor winked.

"Thank you, doctor." Joe smiled.

"I'll sign the release papers and you should be on your way home this afternoon." He nodded and walked out of the room.

"Well, Mary, it looks like we're going home!" Anna couldn't keep the tears from forming as she hugged her precious little girl. *Denki, Gott!*

Joe beamed. "I'll go call Taylor."

TWENTY-NINE

Christmas morning...

The crisp air felt nice this morning, but Joe still shivered as he did his morning chores.

Maa-aaa...

What on earth? Was that a goat?

He moved to one of the stalls where he heard the sound. He shook his head. He wasn't hearing things. There was a goat in his barn!

He moved closer and noticed a big red bow with a note attached. He read it aloud, "Happy Birthday to Jesus! Thanks for giving Momma and *Dat* a goat. Love, Mary."

He tried to make sense of the note. Was it a Christmas gift from Mary?

He walked to the house and called Anna outside. "Come, you'll want to see this."

She joined him and smiled when she heard the goat cry.

"What do you think of this note?" Joe grinned.

"Candace said Mary had a surprise for us." She smiled and shrugged. "I guess this is it."

"Wow! That girl never ceases to amaze me."

"Let's go see if she's up yet."

They entered Mary's room, where she sat up in bed rubbing her eyes. Little Joe and Mandy still slept soundly in their own beds.

A *maa-aaa* sounded from outside and Mary gasped. She flew to the window and peeked out. She turned to her parents with a grin that filled half her face.

"Mary, is the goat from you?" Joe spoke quietly.

"*Jah, Dat.*" She beamed with pride. "Do you like it?"

"Very much. It's *wunderbaar.*" He smiled.

Anna leaned close and informed him she would check on breakfast. "I'll be back."

Joe watched Anna exit the bedroom.

"I wanted it to be a secret Christmas," she whispered.

"Did you know that the very first Christmas was kind of a 'secret' Christmas too?"

"How so, *Dat*?"

"Well, it wasn't a secret to everybody. The shepherds and wise men knew the Messiah had been born. But it was a secret to most of the world and to King Herod."

She gasped. "He was the bad man that killed all the babies! I don't like him. Not at all."

"I'm sure the babies' mothers shared your sentiments." Joseph frowned.

"Why was he so mean?"

"He was scared that Jesus would grow up and steal his throne."

"Jesus would never steal anything!"

"I know that and you know that, but Herod didn't. He didn't know that Jesus came to die for our sins as a man and to rise from the dead." He rubbed his beard. "And King Herod wanted to kill him. But since he didn't know which baby was Jesus, he just killed all the baby boys."

Mary frowned. "That's sad. I bet their mommies cried lots."

"I'm sure they did. Their daddies probably cried too."

She shook her head. "Daddies don't cry!"

"Sure they do. Not as much as mommies, but they still cry once in a while."

"For sure and certain?"

Joseph nodded.

"*You* even cry too?" Her doubtful expression told him she wasn't convinced.

"I do."

Mary's face scrunched up as though trying to picture her father shedding tears. "How come I've never seen you cry?"

"Well, daddies like to pretend they're tough. They are the ones who are supposed to be strong and protect the family."

"But you are strong. You have big muscles."

Joseph chuckled. "You think so, huh?"

She nodded adamantly.

"I think so too." His wife spoke from behind him, clutching his upper arm.

He'd barely noticed that Anna had entered the room.

"Your daddy isn't just the strongest, he's the most handsome too!" Anna kissed his lips.

"Momma!" Mary gasped and covered her eyes in half-a-second flat. "*Mammi* said you're not supposed to do that in front of the *kinner*!"

"Oh, she did, huh?" Joseph chuckled.

Mary nodded, her eyes still squeezed tight.

He took the opportunity to kiss his wife again. "Okay, you may open your eyes now. We'll no longer torture you with our display of affection." He chuckled.

She shook her head. "I don't *ever* wanna kiss a boy!"

Anna laughed. "I'm sure you'll change your mind when you get older."

"Nope. Never."

Joseph reached over and lightly squeezed Mary's cheek. "Thank you for the goat, *lieb*. It was a very *gut* Christmas gift. Now I'll have free goat milk to drink for a long time. I won't have to buy it from the Christners anymore."

"Do you like it too, Momma?"

"Yes. It's the best. That was a very thoughtful gift from a very sweet little girl."

"Is everyone coming over today?" Mary's eyes sparkled with excitement. Such an improvement over the way she looked the last couple of weeks.

"Yes, for Christmas supper." Anna smiled, looking forward to their time with family.

"Who will be here?" Mary smiled.

"Well, Harv and *Mammi*, Cousins Jacob and Rachel and their *kinner*, Candace will be here. And maybe Taylor will stop by."

"What about Miss Linda from the quilt shop?" Mary asked.

"Linda is spending today with her family." Anna informed her.

"Now, you need to get dressed if you want to go to the shelter to help serve the Christmas breakfast." Joe patted her hand.

"What about the *kinner*?"

"*Mammi* will stay home with them. But we won't be gone too long 'cause Momma will have to feed the *bopplin*."

"Are we gonna sing Christmas songs too?" Mary's eyes brightened.

"We sure will!" Anna smiled, thinking of one of her favorite traditions.

THIRTY

Candace was glad that she'd agreed to come to the shelter with her father this morning. It was certainly different than what she was used to for a Christmas morning. But it sparked something inside her. Compassion, maybe?

She found Anna standing by the counter, leaning back and smiling as she watched the homeless people eat. "Why do you do it?" Candace asked.

Anna turned to her. "I'm sorry. Were you talking to me?"

"Yes. Why do you do it? All this?" Candace gestured across the room, from the tables filled with diners to the nativity scene in the corner surrounded by presents.

Anna smiled. "There is a passage in the Bible where Jesus is speaking to His disciples and He tells them that He will one day thank the righteous for feeding Him when He was hungry, clothing Him when He was naked, and visiting Him when He was in prison. And they ask Him when did they find Him hungry and give Him food and naked and give Him clothes, and so on. Then Jesus says, *'Inasmuch as ye have done it unto one of the least of these my brethren, ye have done it unto me.'*"

"Wow."

"As Christians, we are called to be like Christ. Jesus always reached a helping hand to those in need."

"Well, you're definitely doing that." Candace scanned the room of needy people.

"Did you know that my husband, Joseph, was once a homeless man?" Anna asked.

"Yeah, my father mentioned that."

Anna nodded. "When I met Joe, he had no more than a crate and the clothes on his back to his name. He learned a lot during his life on the streets and I learned a lot from him. You can never assume you know someone by looking at the outside. Nobody's perfect and everyone can use a helping hand and a kind spirit."

Candace considered Anna's words for a moment before turning and meeting her gaze. "You're pretty amazing, you know that?"

Anna laughed. "I do not think so."

"No, I'm serious."

"Well, if I am, it is because of Jesus living inside of me."

Candace thought on Anna's words. They were along the same lines of what Taylor would have said. Why was it the people she admired most were those who had a devout relationship with Christ? They didn't just call themselves Christians like a lot of people did, they lived their faith no matter where they were.

And that's when it hit her.

She had been searching for forever, it seemed. Trying to find herself—who she truly was. Trying to find meaning. Trying to find joy.

These people had found it. Anna. Joe. Her dad. Taylor. They'd found what *she'd* been looking for—and they'd found it in Christ. She yearned for that peace. That passion.

"Anna? Will you tell me more about Jesus?" Moisture gathered in her eyes.

Anna smiled. "I'd love to, Candace."

A SECRET CHRISTMAS

THIRTY-ONE

"Taylor, I'd like a word with you before you go inside." Harv met him at the door and draped an arm around his shoulders.

"Sure, Harv, what is it?"

"I'd like to say thank you for praying for my daughter. She was gloriously saved this morning. Anna led her to Jesus."

Taylor stopped in his tracks and turned to Harvey. He stared into his eyes. "You're positive?"

"Oh, yes."

"That's the best news I've heard in a long time! What a wonderful Christmas gift! Thank you for telling me." Excitement built in his chest, but he'd need to tamper it down. Just because Candace had accepted Christ, didn't mean she'd want a relationship that went beyond friendship with Taylor.

"Let's go in?" Harv held the door open for him.

Delicious aromas nearly knocked out Taylor's senses the moment he entered the Benders' home. "Something smells great!"

"Taylor, nice to see you!" Joe grinned and patted his back.

He held up the poinsettia he'd brought. "Who should I give this to?"

"The ladies are in the kitchen preparing the meal. Why don't you go say hello and ask Anna about it?" Joe suggested.

Taylor's gut clenched. Was Candace in the kitchen too? "Okay."

"Merry Christmas, everyone!" Taylor smiled as he walked into the kitchen.

Candace turned and met his eyes. Were her cheeks flushed because the kitchen was warm or was it because of his presence? Either way, she looked good enough to kiss.

"Merry Christmas to you too," Anna greeted.

"Joe said you'd know where to put this." He held up the poinsettia.

"*Jah.* The middle of the table would be perfect. *Denki,* Taylor." She turned back to the meal preparation.

He placed them on the table and quickly vacated the women's domain. But not before catching Candace's eye and offering a genuine smile. She'd blessed him with a smile of her own—a smile that now finally reached her eyes.

Yep, she'd surely found something to smile about. Taylor's heart soared.

~

The meal was delicious, but Candace could barely concentrate with Taylor sitting just across the table. She'd caught him looking her way several times and it made her feel nervous. What was he thinking?

She hadn't had any time to speak with him privately since he'd arrived. Hopefully, she'd get the chance before he left. She had no idea how long he planned to stay this evening, so she'd better grab the first opportunity she got.

Joe placed a pitcher on the table. "Would anyone like some freshly-strained goat milk?"

Taylor shot a glance at Candace. They smiled and shook their heads in unison.

"Mary tells us that she had some 'helpers' go pick out the goat." Joe smiled at Taylor and Candace.

"It was nothing," Taylor said. "I'm just happy to see Mary back at home and well."

"Me too!" Mary grinned.

"As soon as everyone has finished up, I'd like us to gather in the living room. We'll save the dishes for tomorrow." He looked to Anna and *Mammi* for agreement. "If the ladies don't mind."

Anna glanced at *Mammi* and Candace. "I don't know about you, but I'm ready to be off my feet."

Candace and *Mammi* nodded.

THIRTY-TWO

Reading the Christmas story from the Bible, singing Christmas carols, and watching the adorable Amish children open their simple gifts was enough to make Taylor's heart overflow.

But the evening wasn't over yet.

The thought of having a private audience with Candace quickened his pulse. What would he say to her? It wasn't like he'd brought her a Christmas gift or anything. Hopefully she hadn't thought to buy one for him either. That would just be awkward.

As the evening seemed to wind down, he figured he'd better seize his opportunity.

He caught Candace's eye and moved his head to the side, gesturing her toward the door. He put his two fingers on his palm and made a walking motion so she'd know his intent.

She glanced around, then nodded, and met him at the door.

"Are you up for a short walk?" He smiled, hoping she'd agree.

"Sure. Let me get my coat and a scarf." She walked toward the back entrance and he followed.

He slipped his jacket on too and opened the door, inviting her to step outside before him.

"Thanks for agreeing to walk with me." He smiled.

She looked at him curiously.

"Harv told me you and Anna had a conversation today." They walked side by side, heading toward the pasture fence.

She grinned. "My father has a hard time keeping things to himself, doesn't he?

"Sometimes." He shoved his hands into his pockets.

"Yeah, she helped me find what I've been missing. I didn't realize that I was searching for something that was right in front of my face." She shook her head. "I'd been thinking on the conversations we've had. Ever since you talked about that emptiness inside—that part that longs for and can only be filled by God—I somehow knew that was what I needed too. But I was scared."

"Of what?"

"I don't know. That I'd lose myself, maybe?" She shrugged. "But I feel like the opposite has happened. I feel like I have actually found myself. Does that make sense?"

"It does. Kind of like your quest to find your biological father. It put together some of the pieces of your life. But finding your

Heavenly Father helped you to find the missing pieces of your soul."

"Wow, that's exactly it! Exactly." She shook her head. "It's like I invited Jesus in and He placed something inside me."

"Yes. The Bible calls it quickening the spirit. Your spirit became alive."

"I never realized how simple it was. That all I had to do was ask Jesus to forgive me and believe in Him. I feel like I have so much joy that I can hardly contain it."

"You're not supposed to contain it. You're supposed to share it." He smiled.

"Like Anna and you did with me."

"Right." He nodded.

A gust of wind kicked up the loose powdery snow, dumping it on them. Taylor quickly pulled Candace in the barn to escape another gust.

"Whew!" Taylor dusted the snow off his own shoulders, then helped Candace with hers. "Are you okay?"

"Yeah, I'm fine." The barn was dark, but the light of the moon filtered in through the cracks and the partially open door.

Taylor stopped removing the snow, but he didn't remove his hands from her shoulders. He moved his hand to caress her cheek. He took a deep breath. "Candace...I—"

Forget it.

Without another sound, he lowered his lips to hers and gently, but firmly conveyed what his words could not express. The fact that she'd responded by weaving her hands through his hair, and moved even closer, told him she shared his sentiments.

As they parted for a breath, frosty air rose between them. He stared into her eyes and couldn't help it when he pulled her close once again. Her lips were soft and warm like a fleece Christmas blanket, and he wished they'd never have to separate. Having her close was like a dream.

He finally forced himself away because the barn should *not* be this warm in the middle of winter. Or maybe it was just him.

"Uh…" He looked up to the barn rafters above them. "God, help me."

Candace smiled, her white teeth reflecting the moon's glow.

"This is going to sound totally absurd but…" He shook his head. "I love you. I want to marry you, Candace."

She gasped.

Why did she gasp? What did it mean? Did she think he was crazy? He probably was crazy! What kind of man would—

"Yes." She took a breath and nodded. "Yes, Taylor, I'll marry you."

"You will? You're sure?"

"Yes, I'm sure! Now, will you *please* kiss me again?"

"You don't have to ask twice!" He pulled her near, closing his eyes as they drifted off into another world.

This was the best Christmas ever! Not only did Candace belonged to Jesus, but she belonged to him as well.

THIRTY-THREE

"**I** left my phone inside. I have no idea what time it is." Taylor admitted as he and Candace walked back to the house hand-in-hand.

Candace smiled. "Does it matter?"

He shrugged. "I guess not."

He winked at her, then pulled her close and kissed her again.

"You like doing that, don't you?" She laughed.

"You have no idea how much. Besides, once we get inside we'll have to behave ourselves." He teased.

"You act like we've been doing something wrong. Last time I checked, I don't think there was a 'Thou shalt not kiss' in the Bible."

Taylor chuckled. "Some might disagree with you. But I certainly won't." He brushed his fingers against her cheek and kissed her again.

"Oh, wow. You *will* make a good husband!" She jested.

"Sorry I don't have a ring for you yet. That proposal was kind of impromptu."

"I figured. I wouldn't expect you to randomly carry around engagement rings." She teased.

"How about if you and I go pick one out tomorrow?"

"Sounds good to me." She shook her head and laughed. "Just wait till I tell my kids. They're going to flip."

"Yeah, mine too." He paused to open the door. "Hey, I'm getting too old to wait years for a wedding."

"When do you want to get married?"

"Today works for me." He laughed. "No, whenever you want to is fine with me. I do have a *little* patience."

She smiled and stepped inside through the mudroom near the kitchen. "We'll have to discuss it later."

They walked toward the dining area and heard voices.

"What on earth?" Candace looked at Taylor.

They hurried into the other room, his hand on the small of her back.

"Well, it's about time!" Harv called out. A spark of merriment lit his face. "Thought you two got covered in a snowdrift out there. We were about to send out a search party."

Taylor fought a smile. No, they'd been quite warm, actually.

They looked around the room.

"Look who showed up, Candace!" Her father beamed.

Taylor grinned. The excitement in the room seemed to take on an electric charge.

"Jackie, Maddie, what are you all doing here? Erik, Brad? Are the kids here too?" Candace stood in shock, taking in the scene before her.

"Yes, they're playing with the little ones. We wanted to surprise you and meet Grandpa Harv," Jackie said.

"He's been keeping us entertained," Erik said, chuckling.

"We thought it would be a great Christmas gift for everyone," Maddie said. "Especially since you wouldn't be in California for Christmas."

Taylor's brow rose and he locked eyes with Candace. He reached for her hand.

"About California..." Candace's happy expression warmed Taylor's heart. "We... uh... have an announcement to make."

Everyone became quiet and turned their eyes on Candace and Taylor, giving them their undivided attention.

Taylor spoke up now. "I asked Candace to marry me."

Harv clapped his hands. "Woo hoo! Looks like I'm gettin' a son too."

Joe, Anna, and *Mammi* shared stunned expressions.

"Congratulations!" Joe finally patted Taylor's back.

Jackie stepped close and pulled Candace into a hug. "Oh, Mom! I'm so happy for you."

"And one more thing." Candace seemed like she couldn't contain her joy. Exactly the way Taylor felt at the moment. "I found the True Reason for the Christmas season!"

"That's wonderful!" Maddie smiled.

Candace then stepped on her tiptoes and whispered in Taylor's ear. "You were right. God *is* the Ultimate Wedding Planner."

THE END

DANIKA'S ANTI-CANCER JUICE

8 large carrots

1 apple (include seeds)

½ lemon

¼ inch ginger root

Wash all ingredients, peel lemon, send through juicer, strain, and enjoy as often as possible!

*All ingredients should be organic and raw. Ingredients may be adjusted to your liking.

Word of mouth is one of the best forms of advertisement. If you enjoyed this book, please consider leaving a review, sharing on social media, and telling your reading friends.

THANK YOU!

A sneak peek at *Danika's Journey*, book two in the Amish Girls Series.

Danika's Journey
(Amish Girls Series – Book 2)

©J.E.B. Spredemann

Chapter 1 - Tragedy

"To every thing there is a season, and a time to every purpose under the heaven: A time to be born, and a time to die..." Ecclesiastes 3:1-2a

Ri-i-i-i-ing. The seventh-grade students at Lincoln Middle School all took their seats in Ms. Harris' classroom. "Alright class, put your books away. Today we are going to have a math quiz." Danika Morales groaned along with the rest of the students. She felt a tap on her shoulder, and a piece of folded lined paper fell into her lap. Danika looked up to make sure Ms. Harris didn't see. She opened the note under her desk and read, *Is your cell on silent?* She quickly wrote back, *Yes,* and then passed the note back to Cindy as she placed her book in her desk and removed her pencil for the test. She felt her phone vibrate in the front pocket of her hoodie and took it out to glance at the text message. It read,

Math is so boring. Danika grinned. Cindy hated math as much as she did. *I know how you feel. I don't know how I'll ever make it through medical school! Can't wait till next period,* she quickly texted back.

~

"**Hey**, Dani, can you come to my house after school today?" Cindy asked during lunch.

She loved spending time with Cindy, especially since her parents owned a nice cottage a block from the beach. Many times the two of them would take their surfboards out to ride some waves, or just sit on the sand and watch the tides roll in. Danika thought for a moment. "No, I don't think I can today. My dad said I need to get caught up with my assignments. I hate homework." She rolled her eyes. "Besides," she added in a more serious tone, "Dad's having another treatment again today. I can't wait until he's done with all that stuff."

"Yeah, me too. I've heard it can be rough," her friend sympathized. "And now that you mention it, I should probably catch up on my homework too." Cindy sighed. "I can't believe my mom and dad are getting a divorce. They were getting along just fine. I don't know what happened. Why does life have to change?"

Danika hugged her friend. "I don't know. Don't worry. I won't change, I'll be your friend forever," she promised.

~

When Danika walked through the door of her suburban two-story home, she quickly dropped her backpack on the couch and walked to the refrigerator to find something to eat. After she finished making herself a PBJ sandwich, she picked up her backpack and headed for her room. *Since dad won't be home for a while, I can check my email real quick and then finish my homework,* Danika thought, as she searched through her backpack to find her smart-phone. She tried to keep her mind on her studies but her thoughts often drifted to her father. She couldn't help but worry about him.

He was at the hospital again today. He had been diagnosed with cancer six months ago and was having another chemotherapy treatment session. The doctors said that the chemo would help him get better, but it definitely didn't make him feel or look any better. When he came home from his treatments, he seemed even worse: he was constantly vomiting, he could hardly eat, and he had begun to lose his hair too. She didn't understand how that could make him get better. It just didn't make any sense. But his oncologist insisted that this was the only way to go, that is, if he wanted to stay alive. Eventually, he'd said, her father's cancer should go into remission.

Danika sympathized with her dad; she couldn't help but bear some of the suffering he was going through. He didn't complain, but she could tell by the look in his eyes that he was in constant pain. She was sure he was just trying to be brave for her sake. After all, he was all she had left. Her mom had passed away in childbirth when Danika was eight years old. Not only did she lose her mother that day, but a much-anticipated baby brother as well. She couldn't bear to lose her father too. Where would she go? How would she survive on her own?

~

Two hours later, her dad came through the door, assisted by the neighbor who had taken him to his appointment. Today, he had come in using a walker for the first time. This was not a good sign.

Danika rushed to him as she noticed his weakened state. "Are you okay, Dad?" she asked, her concern evident.

"I'll be all right, Pumpkin," he answered bravely. "I just need to go lie down and rest a while."

To Danika, it seemed as if that's all he ever did lately. He'd come home from his treatments, rest, get really sick, start to feel better again, and then go to another treatment. It was a vicious cycle.

"Danika, I want to talk to you about something. Please come and sit on the couch by me," her father requested as he rested on their tan sofa. The neighbor had left and promised to come back again when she was needed.

"What is it, Daddy?"

"Honey, I feel like my body is weakening. I...I don't know how much longer I'll be around." He paused, drawing a labored breath.

Tears filled Danika's eyes. "Please don't talk like that, Dad. You're going to be fine. The doctors said –"

"Shh...it'll be okay." Her father's hand gently stroked her thick nearly-black hair. "I love you, Pumpkin."

"I can't live without you, Daddy. Please don't leave me here by myself." She sobbed.

"Danika, I want you to listen to me. You have to be brave. You *will* get through this. Do you remember your Uncle

Philip? He's your mom's brother – the one that came to Mom's funeral from Pennsylvania."

Danika tried to recall the man. "No, Dad, I don't remember."

"Philip is a good man. After I'm gone, I'd like you to go and live with him," her father stated wearily, taking her hand.

Danika shook her head in denial. "But Daddy, you're not going anywhere. You're staying here with me. You have to! You have to!" Danika cried, holding her father's now-limp hand. "Daddy? Daddy?" She shook his shoulder to try and wake him up, but there was no response. She panicked, breathing heavily. "No-o!" She wept uncontrollably, as she realized her father was gone.

Chapter 2 – Pennsylvania

"...ask for the old paths, where is the good way, and walk therein, and ye shall find rest for your souls." Jeremiah 6:16b

As Danika stepped off the airplane and into the Harrisburg airport, she glanced around. Really, she didn't even know who she was looking for, just that his name was Philip and he was her uncle. A handsome man approached her wearing a full beard with a straw hat, a blue shirt, black pants, and a pair of suspenders. She could see her mother's kind face in his and instantly knew he was her uncle.

"You are Danika, *jah?*" the man asked in an accent she didn't recognize.

Danika looked at the man with questioning eyes. "Yes, I am. And you're my Uncle Philip, right?"

The man nodded and held out his hand and grinned. "Yes, I am Philip King, your *mamm*'s *bruder*. *Gut* to meet ya."

"Hi." Danika shook his hand timidly, choked with memories of her mom. *Uncle Philip looks so much like Mom. Oh, how I miss her!*

"I guess you probably don't remember me. It's been awhile. You've grown quite a bit too," Philip said, as they headed toward the baggage claim area.

"Oh, there's my bag," Danika stated, pointing to a large pink suitcase with a hibiscus flower design. Philip grabbed the feminine bag off of the conveyor belt.

"My *gut* friend Tobias will be driving us to Lancaster. We'll be picking up my rig from his place," Philip said as they approached a black car. He placed Danika's bag into the trunk and took the front seat next to Tobias. "We should be in Paradise within two hours."

"Okay. Um...Uncle Philip, do you mind if I take a little nap? I'm kind of tired from the plane trip." Danika couldn't help the yawn that escaped her lips. In the two weeks since her father's passing, she'd been too anxious to get a decent night's sleep. Thoughts had continually swirled in her mind somewhere between the deep sense of loss over her father to the instability of her pending future, or lack thereof. She fastened her seat belt and leaned onto her small carry-on bag next to her. In minutes, her eyes drifted shut and the male voices in the front seat faded.

"Well, here we are," Philip announced as they pulled up to a white two-story in the country.

Danika sat up and rubbed her eyes. "Wow, I can't believe I slept the whole way."

"We're not home yet. We still need to drive to Paradise. Why don't you head on over to the barn and I will get your bags. You can wait in the rig if you'd like."

Danika shrugged. "Okay, cool."

She ambled to the barn and opened the large door. She had to wait a minute until her eyes adjusted to the dimly lit interior. Her eyes roamed the barn in search of the uncle's vehicle, but it was nowhere in sight.

Philip walked in behind her and noticed her looking around.

Danika turned to her uncle. "I don't see your truck anywhere."

"Truck?" A puzzled look crossed Philip's face. He raised his eyebrows and nodded knowingly, then gestured to the far side of the barn. He walked up to an open black, horse-drawn carriage and placed the suitcase in the back seat.

Danika's jaw dropped open and she just stood there, staring in disbelief. Philip escorted her to the buggy and helped her up onto the front seat.

"Oh, wow!" she gushed, appraising the buggy. "This is *so* cool! I've always wanted to ride in one of these things. Did you rent this just to pick me up?"

Find Danika's Journey and the entire Amish Girls Series at your favorite online retailer or order direct from Blessed Publishing. Write to P.O Box 70, Cross Plains, IN 47017 to request a book order form.

AMISH GIRLS

DANIKA'S
Journey

J.E.B. SPREDEMANN